# Déjà Vu
# All Over Again

## by

## Ashantay Peters

**Déjà Vu All Over Again**

COPYRIGHT © 2015 by Ashantay Peters

Cover Art by *Diana Carlile*

The Wild Rose Press, Inc.
PO Box 708
Adams Basin, NY 14410-0708
Visit us at www.thewildrosepress.com

Publishing History
First *Last Rose of Summer* Edition, 2015
Print ISBN 978-1-5092-0414-4
Digital ISBN 978-1-5092-0415-1

Published in the United States of America

**"And how is Sally, uh, I mean, your mother?"**
He wasn't sure why he'd asked about a woman who'd torn out his heart, but too late to call back the words.

"I call her Sally in public, Mom in private. Can't remember how that got started but it works for us. She's fine."

"She didn't have a problem with us meeting?"

"No, no, she's fine."

Jack knew bullshit when someone spun it, and Carlos wove a blanket. He raised his eyebrows. "Really? I figured she'd fight this get-together."

"Nope." Carlos chuckled. "Okay, she didn't look happy, more resigned. Maybe a little scared."

*She doesn't want me around. I can get down with that feeling.*

"You're not pissed with me or her, are you? For keeping quiet about my identity? The band hit crazy big on that first tour. She, we thought you'd be better off out of the spotlight."

Carlos tilted his head to the side, and Jack recognized Sally in the gesture. "I haven't had time to digest the information. I guess you both had a good reason for the charade, and even though I'm not pressing now, I'll want answers."

Icy fingers gripped his gut. "So my leaving did piss you off."

"Not totally."

Jack held on to his coffee cup with both hands, happy his son hadn't walked out yet. Sure, he'd signed away his rights to Carlos, but Sally had been impossible to find after she'd left. She'd made it clear—through lawyers—that he'd only screw up their son, and he'd believed her. Then his actions had proved her right.

## Dedication

Thanks to my readers
and everyone who helped make this book a reality

Chapter One

*Ring.*

"Ring again, you sucker, and you're in the lake."

*Ring.*

Jack Reed glared at his cell phone. He had a song to finish and too many people calling him.

*Ring.*

A local number, and not one he knew. He calculated the distance between his music room window and the sun-dappled water. If he tossed it, he didn't have time to replace the damn phone.

*Ring.*

Hell, his concentration was blown. He may as well answer. "Yeah, you found me. What do you want?"

"Jonathan R. Young?"

His stomach dropped like the damn phone would have if he'd heaved it into the water. No one had called him by that name since his first divorce. He thought that identity well buried. "Depends. Who is this?"

"I'm looking for the man who married Sally Raines Ford in 1970."

*Shit.* The call he'd simultaneously hoped for and feared for years. Someone had finally discovered his secret. "Good for you. You still haven't told me who you are."

"My name is Carlos Young. If you're the Jonathan who married Sally, I'm, uh, I'm your son."

1

Jack's knees gave way. He slid into a chair. "Hold on. What did you say?"

The voice that sounded like his replied. "I'm your son."

"I...how the hell did you get this number?" Not that he needed an answer.

"My grandmother Young."

His mother had never given out his carefully protected number before, but this was a special occasion, one they'd hoped for. Carlos had finally called for answers.

"Is there a problem with me phoning?"

"No, no I...didn't expect your call. Long time, no hear, ya know." Why the hell hadn't his mom warned him?

"Yeah, well, I'm getting married."

"Congratulations. Oh, is this an invitation?" His jaw tensed. His associates knew he used sarcasm when stressed, but his kid didn't. *Focus.*

"We haven't set a definite date, but we want kids, you know?"

"Huh? Not sure I understand." *Blowing it. You're blowing the chance you've waited years to get.*

"I wondered if maybe there are genetic issues I should know about."

"No, nothing out of the ordinary."

Carlos sighed. "Look, this isn't going very well. I didn't contact you to discuss family medical history. Could we meet? Have coffee or a beer?"

His heart raced. His son wanted to see him. Here was a chance to make up for the years apart. What about Sally? Did she know Carlos planned on finding him?

2

Jack wiped his palm on his jeans-covered leg. "I don't...our meeting...I'm not sure this is a good time."

"I'm thirty-eight. Just when do you think the timing will improve? I...I want to meet you, if you'll agree. This is coming out of nowhere for you, but I've wondered about you most of my life. I thought, well, that maybe you'd like to know me, too."

*You bet I would. I've wondered, too. The formal investigative reports I saw on you weren't enough. Neither was seeing you from a distance. Estrangement sucks.*

"Yeah, um, I guess I can meet you for coffee." Idiot. Talk about thinking one thing and saying another wrong damn ass-wipe thing.

"Wait, you know what? Calling you was a mistake. I only want to ask you one question. Unless you're too busy."

He figured he knew the question Carlos had in mind. and he didn't want to answer it on the phone. "Look, you caught me at a bad time. I'm not always an asshole. Where are you, anyway?" As if he didn't already suspect.

"Close by, in Blue Peak. I understand you're in Lake Stratton right now. That's why I suggested a meeting. We get a look at each other and walk away if that's what you prefer. Or, maybe, well, more."

Jack stifled a sigh. Habit made him hide his emotions. Perhaps he wouldn't screw up so much if he faced his son in person. "Yeah, good idea. Meet me at the Lake Cafe on First Avenue in Stratton. Nine o'clock tomorrow."

"How will I know you?"

"Look in the mirror. The Young genes are strong.

You'll see your older self wearing a ball cap and waiting at a table for two."

He ended the call with shaking hands and turned his gaze to the sunny North Carolina day outside his window. His attention remained centered on the conversation he'd just held. The dialogue he'd wanted for decades and screwed all to hell in a few short minutes.

Damn it all. When he'd heard the caller's voice, he knew but hadn't believed his son had found him. Carlos. His first wife Sally had insisted on naming their child after Santana, the musician that had been playing when they met at Woodstock. He'd agreed. Better to name a kid after a hero than a man who'd later disowned him.

He'd dreamed of this day and the best he could do? Bitch at his son. What a sorry ass. He'd better get himself pulled together before tomorrow morning, or the child he'd waited to know would disappear.

\*\*\*\*

Sally Ford looked up when the door to her store, Good Vibes, opened. Her friend and also her son's fiancée, Abby Stephens, entered. "Sweetie, glad you're here. Would you like tea?"

"No, thanks. I stopped by to check on that astrology book you ordered for me. Has it come in?"

"Should arrive tomorrow. But if you're wondering whether you and Carlos are compatible, the answer is yes. You don't need a book to tell you that."

Abby grinned. "I thought I'd check the aspects. See if your man is on the way. "

"You are insufferable. Just because you've found your mate doesn't mean I want the same. My life is perfectly fine." Well, usually anyway. Lately she'd been feeling restless.

"I think I'll cast that chart, anyway. Something tells me you're about to experience a big change."

"You mean like finally getting the grandchildren I deserve to spoil? A wedding is optional, just bring on the kiddies."

Abby glanced at the ceiling. "I appreciate your flexibility, but don't even try to change the subject. This is about you for a change. I dreamed about you last night."

"Really, sweetie, you should reserve your nights for Carlos."

"He is a dreamboat, isn't he? Thanks for pushing me at your son." She leaned across the counter. "Back to last night. I saw you with a man. I couldn't see his face, but I had the impression that he was your lover."

"Dream on, Abby."

A frown flashed across her face. "Wouldn't you like someone special in your life? A companion? I remember our conversation about life dreams last spring, and you seemed upset that one of your big ones hadn't come true."

"Are you sure you don't want tea?"

Her friend shook her head. No way Sally would avoid this conversation. "Let's sit."

The down-filled sofa cushions and bounty of pillows created a comfortable browsing area, but Sally couldn't relax. Listening to the burbling water from display fountains, sniffing potpourri scents, and a few yoga breaths didn't work either. Abby's question had released thoughts she'd been stifling for too long.

She examined an idea, an opportunity lurking

unseen at the edge of her consciousness. Then she looked at her restlessness and determined Abby was right. She missed close companionship. Her last lover had been too many years ago. Perhaps it was time she took a new one. Her small voice, the one that denoted her higher, more intelligent self, told her to stop lying and ask for what she really wanted. She ignored the suggestion.

"Your memory is too good. Fine, I admit I've been thinking—on occasion—about Jack and why our marriage didn't work. I don't know what I did that caused him to leave." She shifted in the chair. "That lack of closure made me hang on to memories way too long. Anyway, I never found a special someone after Jack walked out." She shrugged. "Perhaps I never will."

"Whoa, listen to you, Miss Negativity," Abby said. "You're the one who taught me to watch my thoughts, words, and actions. You've pointed out that we should be careful what we wish for because we'll get some form of the wish."

"Most of the men my age are stubborn old farts who haven't changed a thought in decades." Her inner voice told her to quit stalling.

Abby waggled her index finger. "We were talking about you and what you want. The full moon is tonight. Put your desire out there." She crossed her arms and settled against the cushions.

"You obviously aren't going anywhere until I answer." She'd have to placate Abby. Or finally take action, her nagging inner voice said.

Abby dropped her arms and leaned forward. "Sally, I want your happiness. In my dream, you looked so content. I want to help you as you helped me. Tell me what you need. No, tell the universe. Please."

Abby's words pushed Sally's decision over the edge. She'd gone too long without a partner. The move toward her new life began now.

She met her friend's intent gaze. "You're right."

What did she want? What was her heart's desire? She drew out the mental list she'd constructed after her last relationship ended. As she quickly reviewed the items, she knew not much had changed. She wanted someone like Jack, but emotionally direct, a man who would face trouble instead of running away the way he had.

"Here goes. My heart's desire is to have an honest partner who sees my heart and loves me, who understands my fears and isn't frightened by them, who gives me space because he needs it, too. He'll have a sense of humor, and will love the grandkids you'll soon be giving me." *And it won't be Jack.* Her heart muscle clenched. *Dang, the declaration wasn't supposed to hurt.*

Her friend closed her eyes, her brows scrunched. "So all you want is the perfect man? Sorry, but you can't marry your son. Even if he wasn't related, he's mine."

Their laughs echoed.

Abby tapped her lips. "I like your statement because you're leaving yourself open while still describing the basic criteria. As you taught me."

Sally shook her head. "I had the perfect man, but he walked out. Don't know how I blew it, but I did, long ago. Now I'll be happy with a second chance at wonderful." She steadied herself. "You know, there's an important step I almost forgot." She gathered her courage once more. "I hereby release all harmful ties to my past lovers and am open to the future."

The store lights flickered then steadied. She thought they'd stabilized, but watched them die out. After a slight pause, the lights hummed to life.

Sally's heart skipped a beat or three. Her skin congealed into one big chill bump. The flickers couldn't have been an omen, could they? Um, yes. She felt destiny hurtle toward her. *I'm not ready.*

"Did you see the lights? The moon isn't even totally full. Ooh, Sally, fasten your seatbelt!"

"Abby." Still shaky, she flashed her friend a warning glance. "Calm down. The lights aren't a sign of—"

"Oh, yes, they are. I know the universe will come through for you." Abby stood. "Well, my work here is complete. I've got a job this afternoon. Talk to you later."

After Abby left, Sally melted into her chair. What had she done?

\*\*\*\*

Sally knocked on Carlos's office door and poked her head inside. Carlos replaced his office phone's receiver. His hands shook.

"Bad news, sweetie?" She approached his desk. "You're pale. Are you feeling all right? Is it Abby?"

He jumped from his chair and circled to meet her. "Everything is fine, Mom. What makes you think there's a problem?"

She pulled him into a hug. "Well, the back of your shirt is damp, your hands are trembling, and you sound out of breath. Not your usual appearance, Mr. Cool Cucumber. You must be up to something underhanded.

Unless you're getting pre-marriage jitters? Can't be that, you haven't set the date, yet. Have you? You promised to tell me first, and Abby didn't mention it when I saw her a bit ago."

"No, no date. Abby wants to concentrate on her business start-up. Plus, we want more time to make sure we're good together."

"Oh, baloney. And you know that's a swear word coming from vegetarian me. You two have been together for months. Abby has work contracts through winter. I had high hopes of a grandchild by spring. Hopes you've smashed for next year. Besides, time doesn't matter when you meet the right person."

"We've only been together for three months. Don't rush us."

"If I hadn't pushed you two together, you'd still be dancing around each other." She held her hand out like someone singing "Stop In the Name of Love." "Don't try changing the subject. I want to know what's flipping you out."

"Oh, hell. I didn't want to tell you this way."

Sally crossed her arms. "What way?" She tapped her foot. "You've always been open with me. Well, except for the girls you slept with, and I'm glad you kept the names from me. Not that I didn't know who they were, not in this small town. Other than that, I thought you trusted me. Have I been wrong all these years?"

"Still the master manipulator, Mom. Thanks to you, I got top grades in my psych classes."

She shook her finger at him. "Very funny, but stay on point. What is going on? What's made you into a nervous wreck?"

"You'd better sit down."

She sat. If any words portended disaster, those four topped the list. Along with "we have to talk." "I'm not going to like what you have to say, am I."

"Probably not." He sank into the chair next to hers and grasped her hands in his. "Mom, you were the best single parent in the world."

She could hear a "but" coming. A chill ran down her spine.

"But I've always wondered about my dad. You never badmouthed him, but you never said anything about him, either." He squeezed her hands. "I thought if I pressed too hard with questions about him, I'd hurt you."

She inhaled, but her lungs labored for oxygen. He'd done it. He'd taken steps to learn more about his father. She should have handled that whole situation differently, but when he'd stopped asking for his daddy, she'd taken the coward's way out. Even at five years old, Carlos had her number.

"Sweetie, I…you need to know who—"

He held his palm up. "No, wait, let me finish." He took a deep breath. "I hired someone to track him down. I spoke with my grandmother who wanted to drive right here when she heard I lived ten hours away. That didn't seem like a great idea for an older woman. Anyway, she gave me my father's phone number."

Sally shook her head. Nope, Eleanor visiting would be a disaster. She must be in her eighties and had never been physically strong. Mentally hard as nails, though. Odd that Carlos hadn't mentioned his grandfather. Perhaps Eleanor kept secrets from the prejudiced jerk with the stick up his socially superior ass.

Speaking of secrets, she knew the one about her ex-husband's identity would throw Carlos for a loop. He couldn't already know, or he'd be all over her wanting explanations. Diamond Jack of the Rough Cuts had been her son's hero for years, and Carlos had never known he idolized his own father. Talk about irony.

Her hands clenched. She slowed her breathing and relaxed her fists. "So was that your grandmother? On the phone?"

"No. Her son. We're meeting for coffee."

Her breath caught. "Not here?" Please, Goddess, don't let Jack show up in Blue Peak.

"No, Mom. We're meeting in a neutral spot." He rubbed his neck. "The get-together may not last long. He sounded pissed off right from the start."

"It's not you. I bet you caught him at work. He gets absorbed when he—"

"Yeah, he said he didn't always act like an asshole."

Why had she made an excuse for Jack? Father and son would have known each other all along, but for Jack's career and her insistence on raising their son as normally as possible. That and the strong feelings she'd held for too long.

Finally Carlos would meet the man who'd loomed over both their pasts. This couldn't be good.

Damn it. She hoped the declaration Abby had forced her into making hadn't invited Mr. Heartache back.

Chapter Two

Jack snagged the only private table in the back of the coffee house. He didn't want to advertise his presence, though the local grapevine had announced his return when he hit the town line. He'd been coming to Stratton Lake and his uncle's cabin since age eight, and most folks left him alone. Tourists were a problem, but not his neighbors. The Lake Cafe made a decent cup of java, and the owner was a boyhood friend. No word of his meeting with Carlos would escape except by accident. Still, he kept his hat on and his head ducked, glancing up when anyone entered.

Sunshine splashing through the large windows caught his attention. The light faded due to a cloud cover he'd noticed building as he'd driven in. Sipping his hot drink, he made a mental note to use the metaphorical image somehow. Would the storm from his past clear when Carlos entered? He snorted at his uncharacteristic whimsy. Partly cloudy sure had to be a better sign about their meeting than a raging thunderstorm. He shook his head. What a knob.

He'd been phoning his mother non-stop since the bolt from the blue hit yesterday. She'd ducked him, and he didn't doubt she'd "forgotten" to turn on her phone. She couldn't ignore his calls forever, though he wasn't sure what he'd say if she answered. Other than, "why didn't you warn me?" She'd always said life was full of surprises, and you couldn't prepare for every shock that came along. Not too big a revelation, then, that she didn't return his messages.

Bitching about what he couldn't change wouldn't eliminate the churning in his stomach. Or the muscle spasms threatening to overtake his spine. He'd been dreaming about what he'd say to his son for so long, he never considered that he'd blank out, but he had. He'd wanted to explain why he'd left, to outline all the reasons why his leaving made sense, had actually helped Carlos. To list reasons why his son shouldn't want to kick his ass.

Now he knew that what he'd wanted for years was only more self-absorbed bullshit. What would get aired wouldn't be excuses but real answers to his son's questions. Plus, he didn't know how his son would react to meeting a father he hadn't seen since age five. Two things he could not control. He hoped his knee-jerk sarcasm would take a vacation this morning.

He checked his watch when the door opened at exactly nine o'clock. Jack would have known Carlos immediately, even without the photos his investigator sent annually. His height, body build, and hair color were pure Young. He hadn't been kidding when he said the family genes were strong. Except for hair length, Carlos took after him, at least physically.

He stood and half waved to ensure his son would spot him. Not a necessary move, because Jack was the only man wearing a ball cap in the place. His standing had been an instinctual need fueled by adrenaline.

Carlos paid then picked up his order before making his way to the table. They stood in silence each sizing up the other and then shook hands.

Jack pointed to the open chair. He cleared his throat. "So, um, you're Carlos." He grasped his hands to hide his shaking and searched for a comment that wouldn't leave him feeling like a fool. "Um, thanks for calling. I'm sorry I acted like an asshole, but I had a project under deadline and the phone kept ringing."

"Yeah, my mom said you get absorbed when you work."

"She did?" No surprise. Sally had always known him better than anyone. To be fair, he'd never opened up to many people. Sally was the only woman he'd trusted to have his back. Besides Sally, his manager and the band were the only ones he'd fully trusted. That's why her defection had stomped his ass.

Carlos pushed his coffee cup in small circles. His fingers tapered like Sally's, and he had inherited her forehead and chin, along with auburn highlights that showed under direct light. Other than the telling mannerisms that reflected Sally, this man had Young genes. Perhaps he'd avoided getting the inherent stupidity that dominated the line.

"Out with it."

Carlos caught his gaze. "Why?"

Jack didn't need to hear the rest of the question. "Why'd I leave?" He dropped his gaze, looking into the past. "I was a stupid shit, missing out on you." He met Carlos's eye. "I'm sure you think I abandoned you. Hell, I did-I walked away. No cards, no letters. But I did what I believed…well no excuse. I screwed up. I hope I didn't ruin your life. I'm sorry."

His son sat without speaking. Yeah, he'd only thought he understood how words could fail. Now he knew. What a piss-poor answer.

"You? You're my dad? This isn't a joke?" He looked around. "Or possibly my real dad sent you because he thought I'd like you better?"

He winced. Nice picture his son held.

"Why would you think...oh you mean my name, right? You know me as Jack Reed, alias Diamond Jack of the Rough Cuts. So I can't be your dad."

Carlos nodded. "Yeah. I've loved your music my whole life. When mom got testy about me playing your tunes non-stop, I'd put on headphones so she couldn't hear."

He'd wanted to be a hero to his son, but not from a distance, and not because he could play guitar and sing. He'd been born with musical talent, that didn't make him better than someone less skilled who got on with life the best they could.

Carlos tapped his fingertips against the table, obviously considering his next question. "Why'd you change your name? Did you mean to disown or hide me?"

"Yeah, uh, professional reasons." Actually the change was part of the divorce agreement. Figured Sally would keep her mouth shut about his identity. She'd wanted no public links between him and Carlos. She'd kept her maiden name when they married, but Jack was listed as father on the birth certificate. A name change put one more layer between Carlos, Jack, and nosy reporters. Plus Jack could give *his* father the figurative middle finger.

"I switched to my mother's maiden name, Reed. I never meant to disown you."

His son looked ready to ask specific questions about a topic he'd rather avoid. He held up his palm.

"Let's not talk about that right now. I'd rather get to know you, first. That's why we're here, right?"

Carlos nodded. "Now that you've partially answered my most important questions, yeah, I guess I'm willing to move on. I have a feeling there's more to the story of you leaving."

His son's calm expression pushed him to say more. "My apology isn't enough, won't ever be enough, but I don't know what else to say. Guess I came to terms with you hating me a long time ago." His gesture encompassed them both. "Nothing I can say now, all these years later, will ever make up for my walking away. I'm not gonna bullshit you, or make up stories, but I can tell you I never forgot you. Never."

"I guess I needed, I don't know, to hear what you've just said. A lifetime of hurt and wondering won't go away in a few minutes, but I can't say I hated you. When you're ready, you'll tell me what you're hiding. Until then, let's talk."

Jack nodded, unable to speak.

They exchanged stares. He sipped coffee gone tepid, seeking a way to connect. "Do you play? You know, an instrument?"

"No, I guess I didn't inherit those genes. I always wanted to play guitar, or piano, but, well, Mom and I did other stuff, instead."

"What kind of stuff did you do?"

His son shrugged. "Ghost hunting, protest marches, school activities, swim team. Mom wanted me to be well rounded. She taught Women's Studies until she quit to start a retail store a few years back."

Jack knew that. He'd had his investigator keeping tabs on his son and Sally all along. Now he had to pretend surprise.

"Well, there's always hope any grandchildren will inherit the music gene, right?"

Carlos stared.

"What? You did say you were getting married, starting a family."

"You sound like Mom, bugging me about having kids she can spoil."

"I'd like to meet your fiancée, you know, if you want to introduce us." He inhaled deeply, still shaken with their meeting. "And how is Sally, uh, I mean, your mother?" He wasn't sure why he'd asked about a woman who'd torn out his heart, but too late to call back the words.

"I call her Sally in public, Mom in private. Can't remember how that got started but it works for us. She's fine."

"She didn't have a problem with us meeting?"

"No, no, she's fine."

Jack knew bullshit when someone spun it, and Carlos wove a blanket. He raised his eyebrows. "Really? I figured she'd fight this get-together."

"Nope." Carlos chuckled. "Okay, she didn't look happy, more resigned. Maybe a little scared."

*She doesn't want me around. I can get down with that feeling.*

"You're not pissed with me or her, are you? For keeping quiet about my identity? The band hit crazy big on that first tour. She, we thought you'd be better off out of the spotlight."

Carlos tilted his head to the side, and Jack recognized Sally in the gesture. "I haven't had time to digest the information. I guess you both had a good reason for the charade, and even though I'm not pressing now, I'll want answers."

Icy fingers gripped his gut. "So my leaving did piss you off."

"Not totally."

Jack held on to his coffee cup with both hands, happy his son hadn't walked out yet. Sure, he'd signed away his rights to Carlos, but Sally had been impossible to find after she'd left. She'd made it clear—through lawyers—that he'd only screw up their son, and he'd believed her. Then his actions had proved her right.

"So tell me about yourself," Jack said. "Your life. I'd like to hear everything you want to tell me."

"I remember you singing to me when I couldn't sleep. Not every time. You must have had gigs some of those nights."

He nodded.

"That's all I've remembered, but I decided my father cared about me. It's partly why I looked for you. You did, right? Care?"

Shit. Those questions made his kid sound eight years old. "Is that why you called me? You wanted reassurance that you'd make a good father to your own kids?"

"Yeah, I guess that was part of my decision to search for you."

"Carlos, I've had to quickly size-up plenty of people over the years, and I can say that you'll make a dynamite dad." He glanced at his hands then back at his son. "This will probably sound like B.S., but I walked away to keep you safe." He swallowed his cold drink to avoid saying more.

They sat quietly. Jack fought to pull his emotions

under control.

Carlos broke the silence. "About me. I couldn't pick out a tune, and I can't sing. I followed Mom into teaching."

Jack raised his eyebrows, not trusting his voice.

"Doctor of Psychology. Then, in another follow-the-mother move, I left teaching and opened a coffee house in Blue Peak. The Collective Unconscious Café. That's sorta where I met my fiancée, Abby." He leaned forward. "You're gonna love her."

His back muscles relaxed. He took a deep breath for the first time all morning. Then he bought them each another refill. Looked like they'd be talking for a while.

\*\*\*\*

Sally watched Carlos walk across the street toward her store later that day. He entered as the sun, which had been struggling to break through the clouds, gave up the fight.

"Hi, Mom."

Her heart did a triple flip. She stepped from behind the counter and hugged him long and hard. "Sweetie. How did your meeting go? You did see your, uh, today, right?'

"Yes, I met my father this morning. Our reunion went well. We had a good talk."

She took his hand and led him toward the couch. She wished she'd added more lavender to the aromatic mist she'd sprayed in the store today. An extra calming influence would help. "And?"

"And when you're ready, you, or he, or both of you can tell me why you made the choices you did with regard to my life. I get it's the past, and I can't change any part of what has happened. But it's *my* past."

Her shoulders dropped. "You're angry."

"I thought long and hard before looking for my father. I thought I knew how I'd react. Instead, I'm a combination of ticked off, glad I finally satisfied my curiosity, and full of questions. And shocked to learn I have a music industry icon as a father."

She played with her chiffon neck scarves and glanced toward her front door. "That's a conversation we should hold in private."

"Agreed, and I'm not ready to hear your side of the story right now. Abby's waiting."

"My side of the story?" *How much did Jack tell our son about my insistence on full custody?* "How angry are you?" *Will Carlos hate me forever?* She put her hand on his forearm. "You understand I never meant you harm, right?"

Carlos sighed. "You'll always be my mom. I don't know if I like the maneuverings neither of you seem willing to explain, but I still love you. My psych degree will come in handy, but I know Abby will help me more. I'll get sorted out, no worries."

She straightened, even though her body would rather have assumed the fetal position. The signs were clear. Carlos was regrouping and determined to get his answers. Answers she owed him but couldn't face.

"I know Abby will help. Should I stay away from the coffee house? Not call you?" *Damn it. Why can't I see his aura?*

He shook his head. "Don't go all Drama Mama on me. It's business as usual for now, except I have to assimilate a life-changing discovery. Wouldn't matter if my father had turned out to be a day laborer. I still have shit to work out."

"I'll be here for you."

"You always have been, Mom. Thanks. That's why I'd like you to try and get along with my father if, no when you see each other."

She froze. She hadn't wanted to consider the eventuality of Jack. "Why would you think we don't get along?"

He raised his index finger. "The fact that you never wanted to talk about Jack told me you had strong feelings you didn't want to face. Thin line between love and hate, remember?"

A second finger joined the first. "No one changes their name without a strong reason."

"Third," another finger rose. "Didn't take long to see you both have strong personalities. Meeting each other again after so long? I'm hoping the earth doesn't explode."

He leaned toward her and enfolded her in a hug. "I'll call you."

She shook off her shock and breathed in the familiar scent of her son. "I'll be waiting." Would her long-time fear of harming Carlos finally become a self-fulfilling prophecy?

He left, his shoulders hunched in thought. She remained seated, her hands shaking, unable to understand why her extrasensory skills had failed when she most needed them.

Carlos's words reassured her, but he was not the only person who had some emotional work waiting.

Given his attitude when he talked about his dad, his and Jack's first meeting had been positive. He'd referred to a "reunion," which sounded as if they planned to spend more time together. Visit each other's homes. Have dinner. Share holidays. Her exclusive time with Carlos had ended, and not only because he was engaged. She'd been willing to welcome a daughter to their family, but making nice with her traitor ex-spouse to please Carlos? Not so much.

Selfish? Yep. She knew the day of reckoning was near when Carlos had mentioned befriending a retired private detective who'd recently moved to Blue Peak. That had been her first clue that he planned on pursuing the missing link in his past. She simply hadn't thought contact with the Young family would happen so quickly, or that the tie to Jack would be made.

*Baloney. The Internet guaranteed the truth would haunt me sooner than later.*

The reality was, with Jack back in Carlos's life, she'd see her former husband up close and personal. And that would be an event for which she could never prepare herself.

An image of a young Jack invaded her mind. His choice of career over family still burned, but she'd been the one demanding he walk away from their son.

She'd screwed up. She'd recognized, and tried to ignore, her immature bid for retaliation against Jack. Now disaster waited. She could sense ruin poised and ready to pounce.

Chapter Three

Heart pounding, Jack hit the brake pedal and pulled into a nearby open parking spot. He gripped the steering wheel tighter to stop his hands from shaking. He'd driven to Blue Peak to see if Carlos wanted to have lunch, not expecting a shock.

Two women, one with a small dog on a leash, hugged in front of the funky looking store. The distinctive Woodstock logo, a dove perched on a guitar neck, dominated the store's window. Of the women, only one captured his attention. *Sally.*

He hadn't been prepared for the gut punch her appearance caused. Photos hadn't communicated her vivacity, what his second wife would have referred to as *joie de vivre*.

Sally's hair had remained bright red, and she wore it in long waves. He loosened his grip on the wheel, his fingers twitching with the memory of her hair spread across his pillow. *Their pillows.* Damn, why had she left him? What had he done wrong besides work to support them by establishing a solid career?

The women and dog walked into the store. His ex-wife still had a confident saunter and wore those swishy clothes, the ones that had whet his appetite for a closer look. Better yet, hands-on experience. Yeah, but she'd shown her true colors when she'd deserted with Carlos.

Even her devious actions hadn't stifled his

preference for sexy redheaded lovers. He knew he'd tried to replace Sally and failed. Every single time.

Keeping tabs on the woman who raised his son had been his only alternative. He'd always considered having an investigator on retainer a smart move to track Carlos's development. In case his son would need him to step up. Not that he ever had. But the photos forwarded to him hadn't prepared him for seeing Sally. Too bad her presence could still grab him by the balls even at a distance of one-hundred-feet.

Right. Like avoiding Sally was an option, even if he'd wanted to steer clear of her. Carlos's request had been unambiguous. Their renewed relationship included Jack coming to terms with Sally. His son hadn't specified how to achieve a friendly platform with her, simply stated the deal breaker condition. He suspected Carlos had harbored a wish for his parents' reconciliation all these years. Nah. Too crazy.

After finally getting to meet Carlos, he needed to make one final stab at the life he desired. He wouldn't walk away from Sally again without learning the truth about their divorce. Once he discovered why she'd run, he could move on, find a woman to love, and make the new relationship last. Learn to trust.

Jack pulled his ball cap on low and donned sunglasses. He locked the car and walked toward his son's cafe without looking toward Sally's store. If she saw him, he'd be done before he'd started.

He entered The Collective Unconscious Café and the mouth-watering aroma of good coffee, fresh-baked cookies, and toasted bread met his nose. A line of folks waiting to order gave him time to scan the room.

Two large front windows admitted sunlight,

highlighting the oak floor's warm color. Most of the wooden tables were filled with customers wearing satisfied smiles above their half-empty plates. A good sign for business.

His attention turned to Carlos. Damn, his son had turned into one good-looking dude. Took after his old man in that department, no bragging. If he could drop twenty years, he and Carlos standing side-by-side would resemble brothers.

The last person between him and his son stepped away, and he moved to face Carlos. "Hey, man. Want to have lunch with me?"

Carlos grinned. "I'm a person down today. How about sandwiches and hanging in my office with my dog Henry?"

"Sounds good." He rubbed his stomach while surveying the multi-colored chalked menu items on the blackboard hanging behind the counter. "You know what? Everything sounds good. Surprise me. I'll eat whatever you make."

"My office is down the hall." Carlos pointed to his left. "We'll have privacy that way. What do you want to drink?"

"Better give me a mug of your strongest coffee." He'd tossed and turned all night, replaying their momentous meeting. His son's ultimatum about Sally hadn't cooled his need to establish a father-son relationship, but had given him plenty to think about. Even though he'd wondered about aspects of the divorce, he wasn't quite ready to confront her.

"Why don't you go on back? I'll bring a tray."

He reached for his wallet.

"No way. My house, my rules. Your money is no

good in here."

Jack began to argue then shrugged and accepted the lunch. His second wife had taught him giving went both ways. He walked to the office conscious that the more time he spent in the main room, the greater the chance he'd be sighted. He didn't want to turn his son's life upside down. That's partially why he'd stayed away, even after Carlos had turned eighteen and the custody agreement had ended.

At the office, he scanned the room, hoping for clues to his son's life. A Mission-style oak desk that looked like it weighed the same as the rest of the furnishings combined dominated the room. A stack of books sat on a small table. His son liked to read. Good.

A Border collie abandoned his bone, got to his feet, and approached Jack, tail wagging. Jack grunted when he knelt to do the meet and greet with his son's dog. That fall off the stage during a closed rehearsal years ago had left his back iffy.

"So you're Henry."

The dog sat and cocked his head.

"Glad to meet you, Henry."

Henry lifted his paw to shake.

"Smart guy, aren't you? I'm not surprised."

Carlos appeared with two filled coffee mugs. "Henry knows all my deep, dark secrets. I tell him everything."

Jack struggled to his feet. "Then I'd better get in good with him."

"He's a sucker for biscuits, bones, and chew toys. But don't give him everything at once. He'll come to expect it from me, too. I'll be right back with the sandwiches."

He continued looking over the office. A wood file cabinet stood against one wall, and two straight-backed wooden chairs were before the desk. Carlos would like Jack's Arts and Crafts furniture. This was a similarity between them he hadn't obtained from the impersonal investigator's reports. Finding more in common had been an underlying reason for coming here.

Framed photos on the desk reminded him of the regular photos he'd seen of his son. Jack planned to tell Carlos today that he'd been following his progress all along, but hadn't decided how to raise that topic. Would Carlos think him a loser because he'd watched from the wings?

He'd picked up the photos as Carlos walked in with a tray. "That blonde bombshell is my fiancée. The other you probably recognize as Mom." He set his tray down on the desk. "Abby's looking forward to meeting you."

No hint whether Carlos had told Sally about their meeting yesterday. He'd have to yank information from him. That characteristic came straight from Sally. "Abby is one good-looking woman."

"Hands-off, Dad."

He glanced up, startled. Carlos's grin dominated his face. "I don't know if you should worry about *my* hands. Musicians are automatic chick magnets. That's why I got into the business."

"Bull. You could no more stop playing and writing songs than breathing. Your career was pre-determined."

He stepped back in surprise, blinking at his son's astuteness. "That's a pretty strong statement. What makes you so sure?"

"Former psych professor. Even when I'm wrong, I'm right. That's the part of teaching you learn from experience."

Heart muscles clenched. Would Carlos see his dark side and reject him? He rubbed his chest. Better stop worrying and accept what he had for now. "Well, professor, I came here for lunch. That food you brought in looks damn edible, and I'm hungry."

"Take your pick. I make a mean tuna salad, and the turkey wrap with brie and apple is one of my best sellers."

Jack didn't care what he ate as long as he could share time with his son.

**** 

Sally greeted Abby on the sidewalk outside her store. The short hairs on her neck stood up, a sign that energy ran hot today. She had the feeling that someone watched them.

She scanned the street but didn't see anything out of the ordinary. A tall, dark-haired man in a ball cap headed toward Collective Unconscious, but people entered the coffeehouse all day. She rubbed her arms. The feeling left as quickly as it had hit, as if the watcher had turned away. The warmth on her neck must be from the unseasonable high temperatures today.

She shook off her unease. Bending to pet Abby's dog, Bunny, she said, "Cutie pie puppy, why aren't you with Henry?"

"I'm on my way to drop her off. I've got a job bid for a mural this afternoon."

"I knew your business would take off."

"Thanks to you." Abby turned toward the store. "I love your new window display, Sally. What made you feature Woodstock? It's not a big anniversary or anything, is it?"

"Not this year. Last big anniversary, the town expanded our normal juried arts festival to include live music with a Woodstock theme. Folks came from all over."

"Sorry I missed it. So this display is normal? It doesn't have anything to do with Carlos meeting his dad yesterday?"

Sally cleared her throat. That was a question she had no intention of answering. "Let's go inside and visit if you have a few minutes."

"Sure do."

They settled and Sally sprang to change the topic. "Abby, now that your business is squared away, when are you and Carlos going to get off the stick and set a wedding date? You know his last fiancée Sierra stalled him for years when they were engaged. You don't want to do the same, do you?"

"Jeez, Sally, pile on the guilt why don't you? Good thing Carlos and I share manipulative mothers. We know how to handle Guilt 101 when we see it. Or in your case, Advanced Guilt 502."

Sally's arm bangles clattered when she raised her hand to her forehead. "Me? Manipulative?"

Abby raised her eyebrows. "Thinking of joining the little theatre group?"

"Okay, so I'm impatient for grandchildren. You are planning for children, aren't you?"

"You know we are. Besides, you taught me to have patience and believe that the universe will bring all things at the right time."

"Yeah, well the universe can't move too fast when it comes to my grandkids." She squinted. Abby's aura was nothing more than a dim outline. Was she losing her ability to see?

"Quit studying my aura, Sally."

"Geez, I never should have started tutoring you. You know my secrets." No way she'd admit her ESP was on the fritz. She tilted her head. "Would you like some tea?"

"No, as I said, I'm headed to the coffee house, but thanks. Want to walk over with me? Carlos made a big batch of peach tea this morning."

"I know. I've been meaning to get over there all day." She jumped to her feet and stilled. A shadow of the Woodstock logo, portrayed in clear relief, lay on the floor before her in a patch of sunshine. Fear churned her stomach. No not an omen, merely sunshine and shade.

She deliberately crossed the silhouette and threw open the door. "Okay then, let's go."

Abby headed to the coffee house's side entrance. "I'll get Bunny settled in the office and meet you at the counter. Won't take but a minute."

On entering Collective Unconscious, Delia Johnson, the woman who had restored Abby's gardens, hailed her. When Delia left, Sally checked her watch and frowned. What took Abby so long?

She tapped her fingernails on the counter after placing an order for the peach tea and a cappuccino to go for Abby. When the barista, Chrissy, delivered the drinks, she asked, "Where's Carlos?"

Chrissy shrugged. "I was covering the kitchen until he took a lunch break. Last I saw, he took two sandwiches to his office. Right after he left, business slowed down, or I'd be in trouble out here by myself. Oh, don't tell him I said that. Smitty and I have finally gotten him to give us more responsibility."

"I won't say a word." So that's what held Abby—she kept Carlos company. She picked up the cups and walked down a short hall. The office door was shut. Well, understandable. She'd give them a minute to break apart. She put down one cup, knocked lightly then bent to regain her beverage.

Carlos threw open the door as she was stooped over. "Mom. Um, I didn't expect you." He stood in the opening.

She straightened with difficulty. "Sorry to interrupt. Do I need to start making appointments? I've got a coffee for Abby. She said she had a bid meeting this afternoon."

"No, um, no, that is, Abby is here." He looked over his shoulder. His jaw firmed, as if he'd made a decision. "I've got another guest, that's all."

The expression on his face sent a chill up her spine. She held out Abby's cup. "Well in that case—"

A familiar male voice called out, "You'd better come in. A delay won't make this any easier."

Carlos pushed the door wide and took both cups from her hands. When he stepped back, Jack was revealed sitting in a chair before the desk. Abby sat next to him, her hand on Jack's arm. The dogs leaned against his knees.

The scene imprinted itself on her brain like a camera's flash captures an image in a split second. Her balance shifted, and a feeling like earthquake tremors rumbled under her feet. And like an earthquake, the aftershocks were potentially more devastating than the event.

"Jack." She pushed his name out from between

clenched teeth. Any more words would have to wait until she caught her breath.

"Sally." He watched her with a wary expression that likely mirrored her own.

His body language told her he was one step, or one sentence away from running for the door. Plus, if his complexion matched hers for paleness, they both resembled ghosts in a blizzard.

"Ah, Jack surprised me for lunch today," Carlos said. "Great, huh? He got to meet Abby and Henry. Bunny, too."

Her son babbled. He should be nervous. This scene held possibilities for anything from drama to comedy and all stops between.

Jack didn't speak, but his expression communicated for him. The look was familiar. He'd taken on his clam persona, waiting for her reaction before committing himself.

She hid her hands behind her back and inhaled deeply several times before stepping into the room. Carlos plopped a chair next to her in silent invitation. She ignored his hint, deciding she kept the upper hand by remaining on her feet. Jack recognized her ploy and unfolded himself to stand in a slow, sinuous movement she wished she didn't remember. Figured age hadn't made him creaky.

"Good to see you again, Sally."

She wanted to pull out the snark and reply with something like, "Sorry I can't say the same." Instead, after a nudge from Carlos, she nodded, her tight, dry throat making speech impossible. She recovered her tea from Carlos and took a sip in what she hoped resembled nonchalance.

He'd aged well. Better than well. His hair was more salt than pepper, but his full lips remained hazardous to her sanity. She snuck another look over her beverage. He had crinkles at the corners of his eyes that told her he'd never lost the habit of clenching his eyes shut when he concentrated. Laugh lines around his mouth, but no saggy jowls. He'd experienced plenty of life yet come out ahead in the looks department.

Sometimes rat fink ex-spouses didn't get what they deserved.

Jack's gaze caught hers. "You know Carlos looked me up, right? I didn't approach him first, so you've got no complaint regarding—"

She was happy he stopped, still uneasy about how much he'd revealed to Carlos about their custody agreement, and her insistence on Jack's absence. Another gulp of tea lubricated her throat for speech.

"I'm not upset, simply surprised to see you after all this time, that's all." She was proud to note her voice didn't waver. Well, not much.

"I understand you stood by our agreement."

He hadn't said, "in spades," but she read between the lines. She'd give him his due. "So did you."

"I guess you were right to leave me." He placed his hand on their son's shoulder. "This man would make any parent proud. I'd probably have screwed him up."

Sally's anger stirred. What a bunch of hooey. *She* hadn't left *him*. He'd walked out on his family without a backward glance. Mr. Big-Time-Musician-On-The-Rise who'd abandoned his family and hadn't contested the divorce. Who thought he could pay her off with a one-time check proffered by a lawyer. Acting the proud father role after the hard work she'd done. Right. And throwing implicit blame at her for the marriage not working to top it off.

"Gee, thanks for the praise. Means so much from you."

His eyes narrowed. "Still can't take a compliment, I see."

"I can when they're sincere."

"Sally, I'm trying my best, here." He put his arm over their son's shoulder. "Carlos won't see me if it hurts you." He dropped his arm. "And I won't hurt Carlos."

She tapped her foot. "So now you're the thoughtful father? Caring what happens to your offspring?" She crossed her arms, careful not to spill her tea. "I don't believe you."

"Me? You don't believe I care? You're the one who walked out, not me."

"What are you talking about? You gave the term "outta sight" a whole new meaning when you left on tour and sent divorce papers instead of coming back to work out our problems."

He stared at her. His face turned red. "Bullshit."

"Still the master of the English language, I see." Sally's anger turned to confusion. His anger had roused, but he'd stayed calm. She recognized that as a sign that he believed what he said. Her muscles loosened. She dropped into the chair behind her. "I don't get it. You're saying *I* walked out?"

A quick knock sounded on the door then the barista stuck her head inside. "Boss, I need help. A tour busload of seniors just walked in."

Carlos nodded. "Be right there." He kissed Abby, man-hugged his father, and pulled her into a tight embrace. "Let it go, Mom," he whispered. "He's telling the truth as he knows it."

She'd already figured that out. "Go get 'em, son."

Abby eyed Sally and Jack, quickly hugged the dogs then left out the back door.

Jack propped one fist on a hip. "You want to discuss this difference of opinion now?"

She shook her head. "Not really. I need to re-open my store, try to catch some of the tour bus customers." Actually, she needed time and space away from Jack. He still grabbed all the air in a room.

"We need to talk."

Yep, those four words could strike fear in anyone's heart. She nodded, unable to speak past a tight throat.

"Soon," he said.

She swallowed. "Later."

He rubbed his jaw. "Not too much later."

She shook her head, stood, and left the room. As she'd feared. Her past had come back to bite her butt.

History, usually written by victors, took on a whole new feel when the losers had their say. She'd have to listen to Jack's side of their split, and her instincts screamed that she might not like the tale. The years of conveniently blaming Jack had ended.

What the hell would she hear?

She already knew she wouldn't like the words.

Chapter Four

Too many lost years had passed since he'd left on tour and Sally had walked out on him—taking Carlos and sending divorce papers—but that didn't mean she'd be less fiery.

Damn, she could still go from calm to hot-ass mad in a blink. All that banked passion warmed his reluctant admiration as he walked to his car. Not to mention her challenging blue gaze. She still looked good. Too good.

If he hadn't been living in an alternate reality fueled by substance abuse back then, would he have questioned the story his father told him about Sally wanting a divorce and full custody with a settlement check instead of child support? Or had Sally lied to protect her relationship with their son? Either way, something didn't total.

He shook off the old hurt and reminded himself their story held more sides than a Rubik's cube. More anger and pain than Manhattan. He'd gotten a lot of song material from their split and created a successful career, but the day of reckoning had arrived. Sally would finally have to explain why she left, and he could move on.

Christ, he really was the emotional idiot his manager, Stuart "Mitch" Mitchell claimed. He watched Sally enter her store then pulled out of the parking space and headed for home.

His male ancestors were dead, or he'd be making a conference call to them right now. His mother still ducked his calls, though he had a feeling she wouldn't be able to fill him in. She'd quietly asked for reports on her grandson and never reconciled herself to long distance observance. His mother had come alive after his father had died a few years back. In fact, she'd encouraged him to make peace with Carlos then, but he'd stuck by his agreement to let his son contact him, first.

Damn, but the Youngs kept way too many secrets. He didn't fault his mother for not mentioning the subterfuge. It was probable she hadn't been privy to the scheme.

No, this mess had his grandfather's prints all over it. The old bastard. He'd wanted to continue the dynasty, marrying Jack to his choice of bride and bringing Jack into the family business. A convenient, non-contested divorce would have been his sort of answer.

Jack rubbed his chin. Given Sally's reaction back there, he'd bet his left nut the old bastard had used his connections to push through a divorce, freeing Jack to live the "Young Family Way." A lifestyle Jack had rejected without looking back.

He and the band were in the first flush of success with everything going their way then. He should have been rocking life. Then Sally disappeared with Carlos, and his father and grandfather wouldn't cut him slack. He'd crawled into a bottle, lost himself in drugs and later, had more women than he could count. It had taken months to comprehend that Sally wasn't returning to him, but he'd tried making up for her absence.

He'd used his brain along with his dick. No one would ever learn that the child pushed on him by Glynnis McKinney wasn't his. One doctor's report had snipped that story and Glynnis had disappeared other than an appearance once or twice during every band tour. Sure, the story circuited that he'd bought her off. What other people thought wasn't his problem.

His second ex-wife, Sophia, had learned the truth. Hell, he'd been upfront, told her there wouldn't be kids but she'd thought it was preference, not medical fact. She'd left him for a mutual friend, Grant. They had three kids and the life he'd never been able to give her. *C'est la vie*, as she'd been fond of saying.

He parked in his drive and watched boats bobbing on the water. Regrets sucked. Time to let that shit go.

*Ring.* Damn phone. Well, whoever called had to be better than remembering the past.

"Jack. It's Mitch."

The band's personal manager didn't need to identify himself. Jack knew his voice almost better than his own.

"Shit. You'd better not be calling about planning a tour. I told you. No more effing tours. I've had it." He slid from the car and slammed the door.

"Hell, man. You're busting my chops before saying hello. What's got your tighty whites in a twist?"

"Whadda ya want, Mitch? Tell me you aren't calling about a tour." He scrubbed his face with his hand. Thinking about the past, seeing Sally again, had riled him more than he realized.

"I want to know if you finished the final song for the album. We go into production—"

"It's an acoustic solo, and it'd be ready if people

would stop calling. Shit or get off the pot already. I can tell by your tone you've got something else to say." He let himself into the house and padded toward the kitchen.

"Hear me out, Jack."

"I'll listen, but I'm not promising anything."

"It's Tommy from Steddi Eddi. He's gotta cancel their upcoming tour. The promoter wants the Rough Cuts. Guaranteed sell-out dates. He knows it. You know it."

Jack groaned. He'd consider a tour for one reason only. He tucked the phone into his shoulder, grabbed a beer from the fridge and twisted it open. "What happened to Tommy?"

"New bride. He threw his back out, probably waiting on her hand and foot. Docs are talkin' surgery." Mitch made a raspberry sound. "I warned Tommy his trophy wife would kill him."

Jack's hand stopped with the bottle halfway to his lips. He smiled. Mitch knew how to pull him out of his moods. "I think you said she'd hurt his wallet."

"Same thing. Listen, Jack, this would be a good tour for you and the boys. All East Coast venues, so limited travel. Starts right before Halloween and you'll all be home for Thanksgiving. Whadda ya say?"

Jack took a swig and swallowed before answering. "I say I hate touring."

"Listen, it's a twin bill. I've got this young band, Grant's son plays bass. They remind me of you and the Cuts back in the day. All they need is a good tour to get 'em started." Mitch paused. "You know, like the break you got?"

Damn it. He owed Grant big time. Grant had been

the headliner who'd suggested the Rough Cuts open for him. Then he helped get Jack into rehab. Mitch knew he couldn't turn down the opportunity of helping Grant's kid, a boy that might have been his if life had taken a different turn. Even if Grant hadn't been a factor, giving young kids a leg up was the best reason he'd tour.

But going out would screw up his time with Carlos. "This is not a good time. I have other plans." *Like getting my family back.* "Plus we wouldn't have long to rehearse." He winced, pissed he'd given Mitch an opening.

His manager pounced. "The Cuts don't need much rehearsal. You can play in your sleep. Come to think of it, you already have. Hey, man, at least think about it."

"I'll call the guys for a vote this time, but I'm not promising a thing."

A beat passed without the answer he expected from his manager. Jack lowered his beer. "What's the real reason you called?"

Mitch's swallow sounded across the line. "I wanna talk to you about somethin' personal."

He sipped his beer and waited.

"We've been friends a long time, right?"

Jack held his breath. This wasn't good. He exhaled slowly. "Yeah, a long time."

"I've watched your back, you had mine."

*What the hell?* "Spit it out."

"Jesus H., Jack. Make it harder, will ya?" Mitch sighed. "Look, I heard you're getting ready to do something dumb."

He remained silent, suspecting the direction this conversation headed.

"You can get any woman you want. Why are you going after your old lady, your first old lady, again?"

Jack's stomach clenched. Hell, he shouldn't have confided in his drummer, Tony, but they'd been friends since high school. No surprise that Mitch knew something was going on and where to ask if he needed details.

He kept his voice level. "Sally's not my old lady. Hasn't been for years."

"I saw what she did to you, man. Walking out with the kid and no word. Sending the damn divorce papers to you on tour."

He shoved his bottle onto the table. "You don't know the whole story." *I don't know the whole story, but now I think I should've manned up and gone after them.*

"And you remember?" Mitch's honking laugh sounded. "I watched you shovel in drugs and pour down the booze. When you weren't toked out, you were passed out."

He replied tersely. "I showed up to the gigs."

"Yeah, you played like a goddamned angel, Jack. You made God cry, you were so freakin' good. Meanwhile, every day the boys and I wondered how much longer we'd have you around. All because Sally walked out. Now you're going back for more? Should I make you a reservation at the Betty Ford?"

Jack tried to loosen his jaw. "You're pissing me off. I'm telling you, you don't know the whole story, so back off."

"So tell me, what are you doing? I loved Sally too. We all did. We're behind you, but we don't want you pulling a swan song on us."

He grabbed his beer bottle, moving it in circles against the table as he took a deep breath.

"I'll tell you right after I figure out what the hell happened."

"Okay, man, I get the message." Mitch paused. "Let me know about the tour in the next two days. This can't wait. The producer needs a band in place, pronto."

"Fine. E-mail me the details. I'll call the guys this afternoon and give you an answer tomorrow morning."

"Thanks, Jack. This tour will be a turning point, you'll see."

"Yeah, right."

\*\*\*\*

Sally had a bad feeling about Jack's reappearance in Carlos's life. Well, in her life, too, to be honest. Acid churned her stomach. The thought of him playing a game with her family didn't sit well. Being abandoned once almost destroyed her. Having him walk away again before they adapted to their new situation seemed somehow worse. So, she'd have to find a way to work with him, to allow Carlos the dad he'd always missed.

Questions about the actions surrounding her divorce had been plaguing her since she'd seen Jack earlier today. He'd seemed so sure that she was the one who'd initiated proceedings, when she knew the papers had come from him. That's not an event she'd forget. She wouldn't have walked away from him, not without trying everything to save their marriage.

Well, that was baloney. She hadn't tried to contact Jack, had even hung up on Mitch. Hadn't suggested counseling. Hadn't worked to realize her dream of a solid marriage together with the love of her life. She'd crumpled with the load of being a single mother when

Jack was at gigs. Combining true single motherhood with building a career, along with Jack's burgeoning fame, had exhausted what little hope she'd had left that he'd return to her side, wanting a new start.

She'd figured out much later that her pride had kept her from what she'd considered chasing after a man who didn't love her. Revenge made her insist on full custody. With the Rough Cuts hitting big on their first national tour, she'd claimed his presence would distract and harm Carlos. In return, she'd eschewed child support in a move Jack's lawyer said was a deal breaker. Jack had agreed—once again through his lawyers—to give up visitation. She'd felt vindicated at the time. Now she knew she'd been a coward. Keeping the truth from Carlos had been criminal.

Choices. Life consisted of a series of choices made or avoided, and hers had stunk. She had the opportunity to make amends, and she'd take the chance.

Good thing Jack had told Carlos he planned to be at his lake house until year's end. Carlos said Jack wouldn't tour again, even though the band hadn't made an announcement. He'd said he wanted to spend more time with his son. If Jack went out on tour any time soon, she'd know he wasn't sincere about connecting with Carlos. Then she could tell Jack to get lost and feel positive about her decision to cut him out of her life. What he and Carlos did was up to them though she had a sinking feeling her-their-son would walk away from Jack. And responsibility for that act would haunt her. One more ghost to carry.

Taking potential action against Jack wasn't the only thing that disturbed her. After learning Carlos had contacted Jack, she'd dreamed of her ex-husband, his dark chocolate brown eyes, long dark hair, and muscled arms. And his full lips that knew how and where to kiss.

As if conjured by a memory genie, her store stereo's random play settled on "Black Magic Woman."

Her thoughts turned to one special night from their marriage. She'd walked into their tiny apartment to a scene out of the Arabian Nights. Jack had created a makeshift tent stuffed with pillows mounded into a heap, scarf shaded lamps kept the lighting intimate, and incense scented the air. Santana had been playing. He'd pulled her into his arms, his desire surrounding them like a blanket.

Carlos had been conceived that night.

"Don't turn your back on me, baby."

*But he had.*

She shook her head to dislodge the memories. Jack had walked away from her and Carlos, remarried, later had fathered a child with a groupie. A woman who'd publicly threatened him with a lawsuit before he stepped up. That man, that Jack not the old one whose memory she'd clung to, held her son's happiness in his hands. She couldn't let a careless Jack harm her son's future, not then, not now.

No, she wouldn't keep father and son apart. Carlos made his own choices. That didn't mean she wouldn't keep her eye on their reunion.

Chapter Five

Jack finished his calls early the next morning. The Cuts' bass player had cemented the decision to tour. The smaller venues appealed to them, and none of the arguments Jack used for taking out a better show next year won.

He wished he could have turned Mitch down immediately, but although many looked to him as the band's leader, in actual fact, the group made joint decisions. Majority ruled. They'd started their career this way, and the process worked for them.

Over time, he'd set aside his personal life for the band. Music came first. Grant was a close friend of all of theirs. This tour was a way of giving back, a practice they believed in and followed. After years of putting everyone else first, he couldn't break the habit.

He'd said nothing to them about his promise to Carlos, or even that they'd met, only that they'd spoken by phone. If he'd mentioned the promise he'd made about not touring this year, the vote may have differed. But why take a chance on screwing up what the band wanted when something, or someone, could take Carlos from him, again? This thing with his son was new and not a sure thing. By contrast, the guys had stood by him all those years Carlos had been gone.

Shit. How would he explain this change of plan, and his part in the decision, to his son? They'd been talking about taking a month-long trip together out West. Carlos wanted to see the Grand Canyon, while he had a yen to hit Yosemite, or Glacier before snow closed down The Road to the Sun. Early September now, he could still squeak out a week, maybe two, away before rehearsals started, but after that, his time would belong to the band. Any progress he'd gained would stall. Talk about screwed.

He could hear Sally say, "I warned Carlos you'd never commit for long."

And she'd be partially right. Touring was the last thing he wanted. Not that she'd believe him.

He called Mitch, relayed the decision, and sat with his phone in his hand. He had to call Carlos before the news hit. Knowing Mitch, the announcement of their substitution for Steddi Eddi had already landed on social media sites. He should have called Carlos last night, when he'd already had answers from most of the guys.

"Collective Unconscious Café." A young woman's voice, instead of his son's, caught him unprepared.

"Carlos there?"

"No, sorry, he's out right now. Should be back in several hours. May I take a message?"

"Nope, thanks." He pulled out the card Carlos had given him and tried his cell. No answer. "This is your...Jack. Give me a call right away. It's really important." Not satisfied with one message, he left another at the home number and considered calling the café back. He did, leaving only his first name, no number.

Rubbing his chin, he mulled his options. He sure as hell couldn't raise the topic with Sally. Or could he?

Nope, he'd wait for Carlos to call. He hoped he'd get the messages, soon.

On the other hand, he needed to straighten out old misunderstandings with Sally. If he couldn't get her to accept his role in Carlos's life, the upcoming tour wouldn't matter. He could tour every day for the rest of his life because he'd never have the relationship with his son that he craved.

He pulled up the number for Good Vibes loaded into his phone. His thumb poised over the send button, he considered his rash plan once more. Then completed the call.

"Good Vibes to you."

"Sally, it's Jack."

She drew in a quick breath. "Yes?"

"You know we need to talk, right?"

She sighed. "Yes."

"Are you busy, or can you take time off for lunch? I'll bring food, unless you want to go out. Public dining can be iffy for me." He stopped before confessing he knew she had both a seating area within the store and a small kitchen through the door behind her counter. Carlos had provided those details.

She answered after a long pause, or at least the elapsed time seemed extended.

"You're right. We should talk. Here is fine, at one o'clock. I'm a vegetarian, so if you want me to eat with you, don't bring hamburgers."

"I remember." Shit. He couldn't know that. She'd been headed down the organic path not long before they split, but still cooked meat. A move to vegetarianism didn't come until later, and he'd learned that through his investigator.

47

"Excuse me? Did you say you remembered a practice I didn't have until after you left? Mind explaining?"

"Ah, Carlos mentioned your preference. He said you never forced meatless meals on him, which he was thankful about. We, ah, we were talking about good restaurants in the area." Phew. Good thing he and Carlos had talked about steak joints yesterday.

"Uh, huh. I'd appreciate you and Carlos not discussing me and my habits in future, thank you."

He wiped his forehead. "Sure, sure, sorry. The topic came up in conversation. We wouldn't talk about you. Well, not in a bad way. Or nosy. You know." Okay, stick in the other foot. "Carlos made a passing comment. I happened to remember it. You know my memory for words."

She blew out a breath. "Memories are what we need to discuss, I guess." A bell rang. "Look, I have customers. I'll see you later."

Sally hung up before he could reply. He'd have to organize his thoughts. She wouldn't give him an inch. Forget that, he'd be lucky to get a millimeter's worth of willingness to change her mind about the past.

But then, they'd recently discovered the truth that lay between them wasn't what they'd believed. He wasn't sure he wanted to give up his version of their history.

****

Sally placed her cordless phone on the counter. Would Jack's visit be an opportunity for good or self-destruction? She greeted her visitors, willing to put her decision on hold.

A small but steady stream of customers kept her

occupied until the City Hall bells rang out the noon hour medley. She caught her reflection in the mirror she'd positioned for good Feng Shui. Shoot, Jack would be here soon, and she looked a wreck.

Hands shaking, she reached for her handbag and pulled out her favorite lipstick. A few dabs over her lips gave her pale face much needed color. She fluffed her hair and evaluated her appearance in the mirror.

She inhaled and shook her head, simultaneously releasing a long sigh. What she needed more than an instant makeover and ten-pound weight loss was peace and calm. And she knew how to obtain both. A quick swipe of blush preceded her walk to her reading area where she sat and folded her hands together. Several deep breaths later, she felt her blood pressure drop.

Twenty minutes passed. A light meditative state had restored her equanimity. She reviewed her options regarding the upcoming interview. Good thing they were meeting on her turf. She needed every advantage she could get.

Let's see. The one thing she couldn't be was warm and welcoming. She'd have to squelch her normal response to life. Her choices might be more limited than she'd like.

Okay, then friendly, polite, and a tad distant, as if he were a stuck-up tourist who didn't know why he'd entered her store. That could work.

Or perhaps her professor persona needed resurrection. Knowledgeable, a bit stern because Jack hadn't done his homework. Hmm. A definite possibility.

Inquisitive, yep, that could work. A sort of, why did he bother to see her when they both knew the truth about their past? Coupled with polite and distant. Yep, she had her approach. She could put on that mask and use it. No problem.

The door chime sounded. Her mask crumpled and fell away when Jack walked in carrying a soft-sided cooler and a large thermos. Dang. His scared little boy expression grabbed her heart. She wished it didn't affect her.

"Hey." He scanned the store then returned his gaze to hers. "Nice place. Smells good in here."

She stood silent, her answer stuck somewhere behind her tonsils.

He lifted the cooler and thermos. "Food and drink. Where should I put them? You still have time to meet, right?"

His hesitancy walloped the snarky comment that floated in her thoughts. She cleared her throat and pointed to her seating area. "Here."

He walked toward her, his normal fluid grace hitched. His aura showed a dark gray along his spine. Either stress or an old injury, she figured. Not her business. She held enough stress for the entire town right now.

Placing the food and drink on the table, he lowered himself onto the couch, leaving her a choice. She could sit next to him there or across the table in a club chair. Or keep standing. No brainer.

"I have plates and flatware in the back. I'll go get them. Be right back."

"Relax. I brought everything. You shouldn't have to clean up when I'm the one who pushed for this meeting."

Crap. His thoughtfulness threw her. She needed to

think. "I forgot to lock the door. Be right back."

The short walk didn't give her the emotional space she needed. She flipped the "Open" sign to "Closed," her hands fumbling the simple act. Taking several deep breaths, she returned to face her past. To the man who hadn't moved to unpack the cooler. Huh. Maybe he wasn't so considerate after all.

She sank into the club chair. "Want me to unpack?"

He grimaced. "Please. I'm a little stiff today."

She spoke without thinking. "Your back, right?"

He stilled. "Why do you say that?"

"I can see it. You know, in your aura. It's gray, like an old injury or something." He flinched. "Could be an alternative timeline, you know, what people refer to as a past life, though that's not strictly correct. Time loops and everything happens...never mind. I forgot you're not interested in my philosophies."

"My brain won't fall out if I leave my mind open."

"Really? Well, that's not what I remember. You always called my spiritual studies baloney."

"I think I said they were bullshit." He rubbed his jaw. "People change."

"Right. Guess they do." She hadn't expected this tack. Blinking, she busied herself pulling items from the cooler. "So, let's see what you brought for the showdown."

He leaned forward, grunting. "It's not a showdown, at least, that's not what I want. I hope you'll listen, that's all. I think we've been operating in the dark for a long time, and I'd like to break on through."

"Paraphrasing a Doors' song? You don't play fair, do you?" She looked up and saw his familiar quick grin.

"Whatever works to get the truth, Sally."

Their gazes met and held. Instant tension, mixed with an odd yearning filled the space between them.

His expression grabbed her attention. Her pulse leapt. She looked away, certain she hadn't seen honest regard—had that been pity?—in his eyes. He said he wanted to clear the air, nothing more. He'd made it clear Carlos's request for them to get along was his underlying motive. Nope, she wouldn't get fooled again. Not by a fleeting glance or by words spun by a master lyricist.

With concentrated effort, she turned her attention back to the table. Not looking at Jack, she asked, "Would you like tea? Won't take more than a few minutes." *And will give me the opportunity to learn how to breathe again.*

"I stopped for coffee." Jack slowly moved to perch at the edge of the sofa cushion. "Here, let me help."

Their hands brushed. A familiar energy rush hit her. The old magic remained between them. No…just…no good. She pulled her hand away, hoping he hadn't noticed the same tingles. She wanted to run away but settled for a diversion.

"I, um, I like to use real cups. Not that the ones you brought are bad. I've got two in the back." She turned on her heel and hurried to her kitchen. Leaning against the counter, she gulped for air. Her first breath caught in her throat. The second made it halfway to her lungs. She continued inhaling until her pulse settled down and her breaths evened out.

"Sally? Everything okay?"

Well, shoot. His even tone told her he hadn't been

affected as she had. She took another deep breath. "Sorry, got sidetracked. Be right back."

When she returned, Jack had opened all but one of the containers. One plate held a display of marinated vegetables in reds, yellows and greens. The aroma of balsamic vinegar made her mouth water. Stuffed celery ringed the display. Another plate was filled with cheeses in colors ranging from white to creamy yellow and orange. Crackers and rustic bread filled a small basket. A large green salad and a bowl teeming with berries completed the presentation.

Feeling composed again, Sally whistled. "Wow, who's your caterer, Jack? I didn't know anyone in the area specialized in vegetarian dishes. This looks great."

"I put this together."

"You cook?"

"Simple meals." He rubbed his neck. "I have plenty of time to try new stuff. I learned the hard way. Healthy eating helps me get through the tours."

Her eyes narrowed.

He maintained an innocent look then reached for a piece of hummus stuffed celery. His eyebrows rose. "What? Do you think I added poison or something?" He bit down. A loud crunching sound filled the air.

The idea that he was nice to her only to get closer to Carlos hurt. Shouldn't after all these years, but the emotional pain hit her, hard. Silly woman.

"Is something wrong? Did I bring food you can't eat? Allergies or something?"

"No, everything looks good. Thanks."

She slipped her pre-determined mask of studied indifference back into place. She filled a plate with a selection of foods her jittery stomach assured her were a mistake to attempt. After nibbling on a celery stalk with hummus, she pushed her plate aside.

"We may as well talk. I can't keep the store closed all afternoon."

He nodded. "Yeah. Guess we need to get this over with."

Wow. Didn't that sentiment make her feel special? Although her last comment hadn't been too sweet either.

"I don't know why you think my opinion is important. I've already said I won't deny Carlos his chance to know you." She poured a mug of coffee from the thermos and added cream, handing him the beverage. She paused. "You do still take cream?"

He sipped and nodded. "Exactly as I like it. Thanks."

His satisfied look gave her pause. "I'll listen, but don't expect more." Shoot. Why had she done that thing with his coffee?

He took another sip, smiled, and inched back into the sofa cushions. "All I want is for you to listen to my side of the story. In return, I'll hear yours."

Her heart beat faster. "What happened? You left without a word, and the next thing I know, your family attorney is delivering divorce papers."

He wrapped long fingers around his mug. His forehead wrinkled then smoothed. "Mitch copped us a last minute gig. Great money, an opportunity we couldn't pass up, but we had to leave the same night." He leaned forward. "You weren't home, remember? Our flaky neighbor watched Carlos."

"I remember." She'd never forgotten the details of that night. "Work ran late."

"I ran in and packed what I needed. I left you a note." He held up his hands, palms out. "I know—notes aren't enough."

She refrained from making a wifely-sounding comment. Or from telling him she'd kept that note for way too long before finally tossing it.

"I left a message for you at work. When you didn't call back, I figured you were still ticked off at me." He caught her eye. "We had a hell of a last fight."

She gulped. "Jobs. Money. We both said harsh things."

He nodded. "I'd called Mom and asked her to watch out for you. She must have said something to my father, because he showed to stop me from going on tour." He stared at Sally. "Being in a band didn't fit the Young life plan." He dropped his head, looking at his hands.

"Why didn't you tell me this before?"

"When I called from the road, no one answered. I wasn't too worried at first, I figured you were out, and I'd catch up with you later." He swallowed. "Then the divorce papers came."

She shook her head, in part to help her thoughts settle. "Wait a minute. Something's not making sense. You signed papers to start the process. The proceedings couldn't have been much of a surprise."

He stared at her. "I saw your signature, my slot was empty. My father told me—"

"Oh, the fountain of truth in human form."

Jack grimaced and she was sure the look hadn't been caused by a back twinge. "Your father always hated Carlos and me. We 'lowered his social status.' How could an innocent little kid hurt his precious reputation?"

He nodded. "He placed social rank first in everything." He paused and looked at her, eyebrows raised.

Once again, her ability to read auras wasn't working. Figured. His tone sounded honest, as did his story. She'd have to wing it.

"I apologize. I promised I'd listen." She rolled her hand in a go ahead motion.

"Dad told me you wanted the divorce, and you'd asked for a settlement in lieu of support and no contact. Total isolation. You were a private person, so made sense to me. He said if I tried to see Carlos, you'd have me up on charges as an unfit father and get full custody anyway."

Sally looked at the ceiling and snorted. "And you believed him? Me, with no money for a lawyer in a custody fight with a wealthy family? Give me a break."

"No, *you* give *me* a break. I couldn't find you. The neighbors didn't know where you'd gone, your dad wouldn't tell me anything when I called him, and you'd quit your job. What would you have thought? Add on the pressures of the band hitting big, my first national tour, and being miles away. I was frantic."

"I saw a photo of you. You were in the background, but it was you and you didn't look frantic. Unless it was frantic to pull off that groupie's clothes." She bit her lip and turned her face away. Shoot, she'd sounded jealous. Time to move on. "That photo made it easy for me to believe your father's attorney when he delivered the divorce papers. He said you wanted a life. No strings." Sally paused. "How could you give up your son?"

"I thought you didn't want me, us. I couldn't bear to see you, and I didn't want to put Carlos through a court battle." His response sounded bitter. "Besides, I understood you had plenty of money to make it easier."

And no child support payments meant he could disappear, as he wanted. *As if I'd never existed.*

He edged back under the force of her glare.

"Money? You sound like your father's attorney. I tore up the check he handed me right after he told me you wanted a career not a family. He said I could have sole custody in lieu of support because you didn't want to be held back." Sally hugged herself. "Sure, stupid move, but the idea of taking that check ticked me off. Like Carlos was second-class merchandise your father was sending back for a refund. My folks helped out. Yeah, we could have used some money along the way, but never pay-off cash. I found ways to provide for and keep Carlos whole without taking bribes."

Jack's arm muscles contracted. "I sold my soul and walked away because I thought that would keep him safe." He paused, regarding her. "Do you want to keep trading barbs or is there a chance we can find neutral territory? Carlos really wants us to get along."

Sally's breath left her in a whoosh. "I don't know what to say. You've given me a whole new version of what happened."

His story sounded plausible, honest. Her hands shook. She needed time and space to reflect, to bring her whirling emotions under control. She couldn't think when her world tilted and none of her beliefs seemed valid. "Look, we've both changed. You're rich and famous and I'm...not. I can't see common ground right now."

They sat quietly until Jack broke the silence.

"Money isn't the issue. We have similarities that you don't want to see. Don't you wonder how our lives would have differed?"

Her eyes widened. She knew where he headed but didn't want to admit she'd wondered, as well.

"I've speculated on how my life would have gone if you hadn't left," Jack said. "Sure, we may have gotten divorced anyway, but in our own way. We may have stayed friends."

"I'm not a time machine experiment, and Carlos deserves a devoted father, not someone who'll pack up and leave when times get rough. Or for a big tour."

"All I'm asking for is an opportunity and an open mind. I'll show you I mean to make up time with Carlos. Do my best to be a father to him, and if you allow, be a friend to you. Tours, well, that's part of the industry, even though I don't want to go out anymore."

He leaned forward, reached for her hands.

"You, you and Carlos, are parts of my life ripped away by deceit, cowardice, and inaction. Mine not yours. I *need* time with my son. I'd *like* time with you."

She blinked but didn't speak. She felt his trembling, or maybe hers. "I told you I wouldn't stand in your way. But the first time you hurt Carlos, your ass will be mine, and not in a good way."

"About that. I've left messages for Carlos. If you see him, please have him call me immediately. It's important."

She wondered why stress lines wrinkled his forehead. "I promise."

"Something's come up...never mind. I need to tell Carlos first." He pushed to his feet. "I want you to know what's happening. How about dinner? Tonight? Tomorrow night? I think we have more to discuss."

"I'll have to check." Right. Like she didn't already know both evenings were free.

Jack handed her a card. "These are my private numbers." He hesitated. "I hope I'll hear from you."

She watched him leave, her worries mounting. Her son would get hurt, dinner with Jack was a mistake, and she couldn't stop disaster from happening.

Chapter Six

Shit. What had he done? Preparing lunch for Sally? Asking her to dinner? Wondering out loud how their lives might have been different?

Had he lost his frigging mind? He'd wanted to establish common ground with her to please Carlos, but he'd gone way past social pleasantries. He'd better back off until he saw signals that she wouldn't cut him off at the knees again.

He pulled up the memory of Sally's face when he'd walked into her store. That little girl lost expression had stretched his nerves like a too-tight guitar string. She'd looked like she hadn't known what to say. The woman he remembered would never have been at a loss for words.

She'd looked surprised when he told his side of the story, then lost, as if every belief she'd built her life on had been proven wrong. He knew the feeling.

Sally hadn't left him, and he didn't know where to take that knowledge. The fact that she still sparked a physical reaction when she touched him was not welcome knowledge. But, damn, she almost looked better now than she had when they'd been married. She didn't take any shit from him, either. No surprise there. He'd loved that about her from day one.

He caught his breath. Love was not a word he'd used in reference to his ex-wife for a long time. He'd determined his inability to stick with another relationship had roots in his unresolved anger with Sally. Keeping his first marriage a secret hadn't been the smartest thing he'd ever done. By covering up Sally's existence, he'd never been able to exorcise her. Now he had a chance to push her from his mind.

The suspicion she still meant something to him was inconvenient, that's all. Right, like he hadn't noticed the physical awareness she generated.

An ability to dissect his feelings and put them into song had helped him deal with life, but the familiar skill left him feeling jumpy. Truth was, he hoped she'd call him and agree to dinner.

Damn if he didn't look forward to seeing her again.

****

"Hey, um, Jack. You looking for me?"

Carlos still couldn't say "Dad" rather than Jack. Well, he stuttered over "Son," so they were even. "Yeah, I have some bad news."

"You're going on tour." His son's voice sounded flat but not angry.

"Shit. Did you hear something? I'd wanted to tell you first."

"Abby and I were in one of the box stores when the announcement simultaneously flashed onto about twenty large screen televisions. Kinda hard to miss."

"I'm sorry you learned it that way. I thought I'd have time to tell you personally." Damned efficient Mitch. He knew he should have called his son last night, but he'd put off giving bad news, a stupid shit decision. He hadn't learned much over the years.

"Yeah, well. I get that music is your business. Sometimes stuff happens you can't foresee."

Shit. He recognized that intonation. Carlos's response reminded him of when his father cancelled last minute or pulled a no show when Jack had a recital or school game. He spoke the words he'd always wanted to hear from his dad.

"I screwed up. I made a promise and I intend to stick by it as best I can. I'm sorry we won't have as much initial time together as I'd like, but after this tour ends, you and Abby, and creating an honest relationship with you take precedence."

"Yeah, well, I understand the band comes first. You've known them a lot longer than you have me."

Jack's chest hurt. He hadn't planned on reliving his own childhood, but could be that was part of healing this mess he'd made years ago. "Yeah, that's partly true, but words don't count for much, do they? I'll prove what I mean, even if it takes the rest of my life."

Silence.

"Carlos? You there?"

"Yep. You want to prove your words? I'm thinking we could take a quick trip together if you can get away for a few days. Abby's got several big jobs, and she wants me to get lost. Says I screw up her priorities." He laughed. "I do that on purpose, and she knows my methods."

"You still want to go? Sweet! Will two weeks out of her hair be long enough?"

"Two weeks is perfect. Business picks up after school starts. I'd like to be back before midterms hit. I told you I mentor some of the psych students, right?"

"Yeah, you said teaching involved too many politics, but you wanted to keep your hand in. I'm proud of you for that." Those words hadn't been so hard to say. Why had he never heard encouraging comments from his father and grandfather? "Seeing as I screwed up, let's go to your pick, the Canyon. Ride down to that ranch on mules, or go river rafting. Whatever works."

"Sounds good. When can you leave?"

"Soon as you can." He rubbed his neck. "Hey, one more thing."

"Is there a problem?"

His nervousness about his next request must have communicated the wrong message to his son. "No, I...you know, thought you'd like to come see me when the Cuts play Charlotte. You and Abby. Your mom, too, if she wants." He cleared his throat. "Because, you know, you said you liked the band, and I want you to meet them."

He paused, unsure if their call had been cut off.

"Carlos?"

"You're kidding, right? You'd get us seats? I heard the tour sold out in less than an hour after tickets went on sale this morning."

"You can have first row center if you want, but I'd planned all access passes. Sit in on sound check. Join us in the Green Room. Hang in the wings." He didn't hear a response. "Or not. I want to show you some of my world."

"Holy shit. Abby's not gonna believe this. We'll take those all access passes. I'll make a hotel reservation right after we hang up."

"You can stay with me. Mitch always books two whole floors. For privacy." He often shared a two-bedroom suite with Tony in case they were too wired to sleep and wanted to work. Tony wouldn't mind moving for the night.

"Wow. Abby will flip."

"You know it'd be better not to tell anyone else, right? I'd like our relationship to stay under the radar until we're more comfortable together."

"Hell, there go my plans for expanding the coffee house. I figured the extra business I'd pull in from the media crush when everyone learned about your secret son would be good for another thousand square feet or so. I thought about serving dinner, adding more employees."

Jack stilled. He hadn't figured Carlos for a user. Not that he'd mind spending every dime he had if it meant he'd have a chance to help his son. But if anyone understood money couldn't guarantee happiness, he did.

Carlos laughed. "Joking. If I can't make a success on my own, I'm not your son."

"You sounded like your grandfather for a minute. No, cancel that. You sound like you. You'll mention the invitation to your mom, right? I don't want her to feel left out." Christ. Why did he push this? He had a strong feeling Sally would prefer him totally out of the picture. Well, tough. He was back and back to stay.

"Why don't you ask her? You agreed to fix things between you."

"It'll sound better coming from you. I don't want to push her."

"I get it. I'll ask her."

"Okay, good. So, you're not ticked off? About the trip west, or my tour coming out of nowhere? Or anything else?"

"Well, I wasn't too happy to see the news on

television, you know, I thought you were gonna be honest with me. All of us."

"I see." Jack floundered for words.

"But, you live in a different world. One I can't understand right now. So, I'll give you a break about our lack of communication."

"Thanks." Jack's breathing eased.

"You can thank Abby. She's got a handle on difficult parents." Carlos inhaled noticeably. "I mean—"

"You meant what you said. No apologies. I'm glad you want to move on, and I promise to do better from now on."

"Okay. I can accept that. I'd better get on-line to see what kind of last-minute arrangements we can make for Arizona."

"Don't bother. That's what I pay a personal business manager to handle. He's got a staff member who can handle our trip in less time than it'd take you to pull up the first website." Cathy would pull strings to get them the best accommodations available.

"Wow. I can see getting to know you will open some doors."

This time Jack heard the humor. "Yeah, the door to the men's room."

When their shared laugh died out, he continued. "By the way, our first trip is played by my rules. You aren't paying a dime."

"Hell, that's not fair. I'm almost forty not some little kid waiting for summer vacation. I can pay my own way."

"I know that. I want to do this."

"Fine, okay. Thanks."

Jack released the breath he'd held. "Good. I'll get back with you later today. We should have an itinerary by then."

"You don't mess around, do you?"

"Life is short, son. Way too short."

\*\*\*\*

Sally watched Carlos cross the street, the wind whipping his brown hair into peaks. He looked like he couldn't decide between punching his fist in the air to celebrate or shuffling slowly to delay his visit to the principal's office. He entered on a bounce.

"Hey, sweetie. How's business?"

"Slow right now so I thought I'd come visit my favorite mom."

She withdrew from his long hug. "I'm your only mom, you goof. Unless you have another one hidden away?" Crap, had Jack married again and she'd missed the news? Perhaps Carlos referred to a stepmother. She needed to remember she wasn't his only recognized parent any more.

He flicked a glance over her shoulder, avoiding her eyes.

"Do you have time to sit and tell me the real purpose of your visit? Or do I have to call Abby?"

"Geez, make me feel like a ten-year-old."

"If that's what you want, sure. Otherwise, spill it." She tilted her head and examined his expression. "Wait, are you here to tell me you've set a wedding date?" She squealed. "Oh, that's it, isn't it? Well, come on, give. When is it? Where? Who's standing up? This is so exciting!"

He ducked his head. "No, Abby and I haven't set a date, but we will, soon."

Her on again, off again aura reading kicked in this time. He kept a secret. Not a problem. She'd worm the information out of Abby later today. These two didn't realize whom they tried to fool.

They sat. "So, spill. What's up?"

He took her hand in his. "You know I've talked about taking time to get to know Jack, right?"

Sally nodded, fighting to keep her expression blank.

"Yeah, so we're going out West for two weeks. We're headed for the Grand Canyon." He bounced like the ten-year-old he didn't want to be considered. "I've been wanting to visit there for years."

"That's great, honey." Her words didn't sound forced, a surprise given her tight jaw. "When are you leaving? Is Abby going along?"

"Naw, Abby wants me gone so she can concentrate on her first major commission outside of Blue Peak. We wouldn't see much of each other anyway, so this is good timing. Plus we have to fit in the trip before the tour."

"Tour? You and Abby are planning to travel for a while?" She pulled her hand from his. "No, stupid me, you mean before Jack and the band go out again. I thought he'd finished with that scene." She crossed her arms. "Figures he'd break his promise."

Of all the nasty tricks to play, Jack had laid a real trip on them. Had he been honest about the divorce? Blaming it on his father...no, he'd taken responsibility for his actions, even after the fact. Still, he was abandoning Carlos again. The rat face. Or...could be that's what he'd stopped by to tell Carlos earlier today. And what he planned to explain to her over dinner.

Carlos hugged her. "He's not walking away. He apologized for not telling me sooner and suggested we still hang together." He caught her gaze. "He can't help the circumstances, Mom. I believe he's trying hard."

"I suppose."

"Don't suppose, ask those mystical guides of yours for the truth. Besides, when they play Charlotte, Abby and I are going and hanging with the band."

"You're what?" She had to remind herself Carlos was grown, that the band had lost its party-hearty reputation, and that Jack wouldn't knowingly put his son in jeopardy. Still, the fact her ex could provide for Carlos in a way she couldn't, hurt. She disliked her pettiness, but sometimes the tough spiritual work she'd done didn't stick worth a damn.

"You heard me. And you're invited, too. I didn't know if you'd want to see the Cuts, so I didn't accept for you. But I'll be talking with um, Jack tonight. He said he'd like you there if you want." Carlos bounced again. "Full access passes, a hotel room on his private floor, the works."

She narrowed her eyes. Her son had a secret. Well, more than one, but he held some vital detail back. Probably the lie about Jack wanting her along.

Her hands shook. Could she see the band again? She'd avoided the "news" splayed across the tabloids through the years. To go from almost no exposure to full immersion—up close and personal—could pose some huge problems. Or perhaps the opportunity would allow her to heal more relationships and move on without pain. "I'll think about it and let you know. Do you need an answer today?"

"No, but sooner than later, I guess."

"Fine." She dredged up a smile. "You have some exciting stuff coming up. Good on you!"

"Yeah." He wore a bemused smile. "Who'd have thought, huh?"

"Yeah." *I did. I knew that Jack's return would change our lives irrevocably.* She'd tried to be a good mother, but she may have done everything all wrong. Perhaps she should have insisted Jack make time for his son, told his father's attorney to screw the divorce until Jack returned. Maybe their son had needed two parents, even if one only showed up a couple of times a year with reporters on his heels.

"Sweetie, let me know if I can help you get ready. Will the café have coverage? Do you need to hire and train someone to fill in for you?"

"We should be good, thanks."

"Carlos—"

"Don't worry, Mom. I still love you best. Well, after Abby."

"And Henry. I know that dog acts as your sounding board. Don't worry about your old mother. I'm still hot stuff in some circles."

He hugged her. "I know. I threaten the boys coming in the café with dismemberment all the time. These young kids don't know how to talk about a lady, and you're no cougar."

She rested her head on his shoulder. "Thanks, sweetie."

She put her shoulda, woulda, coulda thoughts behind her. Carlos wanted time with his dad. She'd said repeatedly she wouldn't interfere.

Even if their vacation and concert plans smacked of mom abandonment and hurt like hell.

Chapter Seven

Sally spent the rest of the day and half the next defending her reasons for avoiding dinner with Jack. She knew she should pony up, but later was better. Not that delay had helped her in the past.

Carlos leaned across her counter. "Mom, Jack told me he invited you to dinner. You know you can't avoid him forever, right? So what's the deal?"

"No deal. I understand you want your parents to get along. I'll play nice when he comes to see you, but I see no reason to establish any other contact."

"Crap. You are so full of it I don't know where to start. Abby said the air turned so thick when you and Jack saw each other again, she couldn't wait to leave. The dogs were jumpy all afternoon. And you're telling me 'no deal?' Really?"

She clasped her hands and leaned against the store counter. "That's right. I've come to terms with your father's return."

"You haven't calmly accepted this situation any more than he or I have. What I have with Jack is shiny new. A different existence, one with a father."

His face lit and once again, she understood what her actions had cost her son. She sighed. "I know I made a mistake in keeping you apart. It's past time for you to know each other, and I'm sorry I screwed up your life."

"I accept your apology—again—and my getting to know Jack isn't the issue."

She understood his inference. Was he correct in his assumptions?

"Mom, it's easy to see you and Jack never resolved your feelings or came to terms with the divorce. You looked as if you didn't know whether to hug him or slug him in my office."

"I thought I handled the shock, I mean surprise, rather well."

"You would," he muttered.

She knew better than to ask for details. "Why are you pushing us together? If Jack and I have unresolved feelings—and I'm not admitting I do—then we have a problem to solve, not you. Stop pushing me."

"I've lived with you all my life, and I know if I don't force this, you'll keep your feelings about my father buried. Forever, if you can. Sorry, but that's not too healthy. Or smart."

"I never thought encouraging you in your psychology studies would come back to bite me."

He grinned. "Yeah, life can suck. So can that karma philosophy you hold."

"Fine." Her response sounded more grudging than she'd like. "Okay, I'll call him. One dinner together won't hurt, I guess." There, her tone had hit a balance between conciliation and resolve.

"Great." He rubbed his palms together. Stepping forward, he pulled her into a hug. "I need to get back. I'm glad you're okay with calling Jack. You'll feel better once everything shakes out."

"Pardon me? You're using my own lines against me now?"

"Whatever gets the job done." He grinned and headed for the door. "Don't forget to call. I bet Jack's waiting to hear from you. See ya." He hurried out.

"I should have known. Give that guy an opening and he uses Carlos to manipulate me." She perched at the edge of her chair. "Heck, that's not true. I'm lucky Carlos hasn't disowned me. Not to mention it was Carlos's idea that we all get along."

She tapped her forefinger against her lips. Carlos rated at the top of the best son scale, and as a teacher, she'd seen the full gamut. He'd never given her too many worries outside of the normal boyhood stuff he'd pulled. The least she could do for him, for herself, was come to terms with her former spouse. But simply because she knew her responsibilities didn't mean she had to call Jack right away.

Looking toward the door, she willed customers to enter and remove the opportunity for following through on her decision. No one arrived, not then and not for the next hour. Tension built, her breath shortened.

"Shoot. All right, already. I'll call." She picked up her phone then replaced the receiver. "What the heck will I say?"

She tried out phrases and intonations for a few minutes. The soft internal voice some called intuition but that she regarded as a higher intelligence took her to task. "Just call." She heard the whisper and knew she shouldn't put off the task.

Her hands shook as she dialed. If lucky, he wouldn't answer, and she could leave a voice message, instead. When he answered, she knew her luck had bombed.

"Jack, uh, hi."

"Hi. I'm glad you called."

"You are?"

"Yeah, I've been hoping, you'd…aw hell. Never mind about me. What's your decision? Will you have dinner with me tonight?"

"Yes, that'd be nice, yes." Sally would have kicked herself but her legs were folded under her. She hadn't meant to sound breathy. Shoot.

"So. My house okay, or would you prefer neutral territory? I could make reservations at Stratton Lake. I'd be happy to pick you up."

Neither spoke for a long moment.

"Unless you'd rather drive yourself," he said. "That would make tonight more a meeting and feel less like a date."

He'd zoomed in on her concerns. "I hadn't thought that far. Give me a sec." She didn't need time to know she didn't want to share dark, private, close quarters with him.

"Neutral territory would be great if we can go somewhere we won't be interrupted."

"I've got the place."

He named Celeste's, an upscale lakeside restaurant known for their innovative chef. Last minute reservations were impossible. Obviously, that didn't concern Jack. Envy swamped her, followed by anger. She fought to regain her composure.

"Is eight o'clock too late?"

"What? No, that's fine. I'll meet you there."

She hung up and immediately dialed the Snip 'n Curl. A night with Jack demanded a mani-pedi and facial just to bolster her confidence. She'd resurrect the black dress and heels that had driven her last date to his

73

Ashantay Peters

knees. This dinner hadn't been her idea or desire, but she wouldn't go unprepared. She had no choice.

Well, that last thought wasn't true. There were always choices. Sometimes the offerings were a rock and a glacier, but the choice remained.

**\*\*\*\***

She'd agreed to dinner. Jack turned off his phone, needing uninterrupted time to think. Carlos had initially suggested Sally and Jack meet to begin working out the tangled past. He'd resisted, but after seeing Sally at lunch yesterday, he'd known Carlos was right. The pack of guilt and pain he carried was larger than a stack of stadium-sized amplifiers.

He wouldn't ponder how much he still craved Sally's good opinion.

"Hey, Pete? Yeah, we're on for tonight. Eight o'clock. You sure your staff doesn't mind? You'll be there? Hey, thanks, man. My mouth is all set for your kale salad. Yeah, later."

Jack and Pete had run together every summer he'd spent at his uncle's lake cottage. They'd become best friends when Pete's family moved, allowing Pete to attend the same high school as Jack. Pete had cheered him on, encouraging him to strike out on a music career in defiance of his father and grandfather. Hell, if it weren't for Pete's getting him to the Woodstock festival, he'd never have met Sally.

When Pete finished culinary school and his apprenticeships, Jack fronted the money for his first restaurant. Now Pete ran a small bistro in an old Victorian home at Stratton Lake. His chef was top notch, and he drew people with his annual culinary weekend featuring wine pairing dinners and master

74

classes.

Normally, when Jack visited, Pete seated him at the small chef's table in the kitchen for privacy. Jack had picked up plenty of food tips and made friends with the staff. Tonight Jack and Sally would dine at the best lake view table, in a homey setting devoid of anyone other than Pete and his crew.

He figured they'd need the privacy, especially if Sally's anger stirred. Ticking her off used to be easy for him, and he doubted much had changed in that department. He put through another call.

"Collective Unconscious Café."

"Hey, Carlos. Your mom agreed to dinner tonight. I have a feeling you were involved in her decision."

"I'd like my parents to get along."

"Yeah. It's the least we can do." He scrubbed his cheek with his free hand. "You're sure she won't back out?" He'd never known her not to keep her commitments, but people changed. He didn't really know her anymore, though his physical response to her sure remained the same.

"I heard she made an emergency appointment at the salon. This town's gossip moves faster than the old Concorde jet. Sorry, I've gotta run."

"Right." Jack placed his phone on the table. He rubbed his neck.

Sally was at the beauty salon, preparing for the evening with him? If this were any other woman, he'd know exactly what that portended. With her, he had the feeling she polished her armor.

A grin stretched his lips. The salon, huh? If Sally didn't care, she wouldn't go to any trouble. She'd show up, dressed neatly but nothing special. At least, that's the way the old Sally would react.

He stretched out on the couch. Could be she'd recognized the sexual tension remained for her, too. That put a whole new twist on the upcoming dinner.

****

Celeste's highway sign indicated they were closed on Mondays after Labor Day. Sally figured she'd find an empty parking lot and Jack waiting with an apology. Given the cars parked out front, Celeste's must have changed their schedule but not their small billboard.

She checked her lipstick using the rearview mirror and then slid from the car. Her stomach was empty, not in anticipation of the meal ahead but because she hadn't been able to down either food or drink since she'd accepted Jack's invitation.

Inside the door, the lack of chatter and bustle of servers made her rethink her earlier assumption. Her eyes adjusted and she saw the place stood empty. Well, except for the approaching man.

"Sally Ford? Your party is waiting."

She struggled to understand why the man's voice and face triggered a memory. He didn't look the type to enter her store. The restaurant had always been out of her price range. Well, not really, but she hadn't wanted to eat here alone, and none of the men she'd dated casually had suggested this as a destination. She must have seen him around town

She dismissed the niggling sense pestering her, focusing instead on the man waiting at a lake view table. Jack stood as she approached. His back was to the fading sunlight, hiding his expression. A wine stand held a still corked bottle.

The cozy scene sent her pulse skittering. She

inhaled through her nose to hide her sudden breathlessness. What did Jack plan? And why had she agreed to this meeting?

She slid in to her chair, hoping her expression portrayed calm. "Hello, Jack."

"Sally." He sat.

They stared at each other. The maître d' cleared his throat. "Shall I pour?"

Jack jerked. He blinked. "Yes, thanks, Pete."

*Pete?*

She focused on the man standing next to her with new intent. "Pete? As in Pete Hudson?"

He grinned and she recognized the young friend she remembered from the early days of living with Jack. No longer a beanpole, Pete had matured into a handsome, self-assured man with a clear complexion, and given his smooth movements, a set of muscles. He hadn't bulked up so much as filled out. His eyes still held the same twinkle she remembered. Silver hair gleamed at his temples. No wonder his culinary classes were always sold out. The guy had charisma plus.

"Yep. I see by your dropped jaw you're remembering the old Pete." He wiped a hand down his jacket front. "I've changed a bit since you knew me."

"I'll say."

"So that's a nod of approval from the still gorgeous Sally? I had a big crush on you back then. Jack threatened to kick my butt more than once when he thought I was moving in on you." He grinned. "I'm available if you want a different dinner companion."

"Really? Slip me your phone number when you serve the first course. I can ditch this guy early. I'd like to hear what you've been up to all this time."

"Balls. Just pour and get out, Pete." Jack hadn't raised his voice, but his tone spoke a library full of volumes.

Pete smirked. "He hasn't changed much. The big man speaketh. Better listen." Ice tinkled as Pete lifted the wine bottle from the stand. He expertly performed the opening and tasting. After filling both glasses, he gave a short bow and left.

She huffed. "That was rude. He's your friend, not a servant."

"Don't worry. He put me in my place, as always."

Her forehead wrinkled.

"That silent act," Jack explained. "He knew he could get back at me through you. Don't you remember? He used to pull the same thing years ago. He'd withdraw and you'd stand up for him."

She leaned against her chair. Her thoughts rattled like a jalopy on a gravel road. She hadn't seen either of these men for decades. Why had clear and detailed memories of them hanging together returned with a rush?

"I haven't seen Pete since—" Since their wedding. She didn't want to head down that beaten path. "Now that you mention it, I thought Pete was shy and sensitive. When he announced he was leaving to study at a French culinary school, well, I kind of thought he might be gay. Although I don't think that now."

A grin split Jack's face. "Thanks, that'll get Pete. Sorry to disappoint your plans for hooking up later, but Pete married a French woman. Celeste acts as hostess. They have two grown kids. A couple of grandkids. She's babysitting tonight or she'd be here."

"Really? Good for him. Them."

Jack leaned forward, his long fingers wrapped around his wine glass. "So, do you want to chit chat about the weather and the view, or do you want to hold a real conversation? Or both? You decide."

She'd always loved watching his hands. Oh, hell. Her wits resembled scrambled eggs instead of a working brain. She concentrated on not spilling her wine.

"You probably don't want to talk about the books I sell in my store, or the theories and philosophies I use to live life."

"Try me."

She tried to gauge his expression but the shadows cast by the last rays of the sun entering through the window made it difficult to get a good read. "Okay, fine. What are your thoughts on using astrology as a guide to making decisions? How about developing your intuitive powers or listening to nature's messages? Have you ever had a tarot reading? What do you think about quantum mechanics, multi-verses and string theory? Is time travel possible?"

He leaned back and smiled. "I'll try to answer your questions, but don't bust my chops if I miss one. First, I don't use astrology, though I understand many people do. I think most creative people have developed their intuition, but I could be wrong. When I look out the window and see dark clouds, I figure nature is telling me it's about to rain. No, I've never had a tarot reading and probably never will."

He leaned forward. "As far as quantum mechanics, I watch *Big Bang Theory* reruns when I can. I figure whoever writes that stuff is smarter than I am, so I'll let them think about all that." He took a deep breath. "And finally, your last question about time travel."

He held her gaze. She held her breath.

"If I could travel back in time and fix my mistakes, I'd do it. Faster than one of Jimmy Page's chord changes."

She stared sightlessly out the window then turned back. Jack gazed at her and sadness flickered across his expression. Did she really want to stir the ashes of their former relationship? She had a niggling feeling there might be some sparks left. Better play it safe.

"I see." She faked a smile. "Then we'd better find common topics and stick with those."

He finished off his wine. "Okay, fine. What do you think of the restaurant?"

"Thanks for asking me here. I've wanted to come for dinner or one of the classes, but haven't."

"I thought it would be a good place to thank you for Carlos."

"I'm pretty sure we made him together."

His lips curved up. "Yeah, we did. I meant raising him." His smile disappeared. "I thought he'd be more angry about my leaving. He's handled my reentry into his orbit better than I have."

"Carlos is low-key and generous to a fault. He's taught me a few things about forgiveness over the years."

"I'm pretty sure he learned those lessons from you."

She gulped. Her scratchy throat made an answer difficult.

As if reading her emotions, he veered to another topic. Their conversation flowed. They didn't avoid controversial subjects, but the need to be right didn't get the upper hand. Sally felt the years fall away, and her attraction to Jack grew as the night progressed. The candlelight, glass of wine, and good food left her feeling like a young girl enjoying dinner with a man she could love.

Love? She almost choked on the wine she'd sipped. No way she'd travel that road again, not with Jack. Even though sparks had flown since they'd met again, she hadn't wanted to confront her feelings for Jack. Or his for her. Now was past time.

"Jack, I don't understand what I'm—we're—really doing here. Is this evening some misguided attempt to rewrite the past?"

"We agreed to have dinner to see if we could be friends, right?" He ran his fingers through his hair. "But, damn, I've been wanting to jump you for the past hour, and I'm pretty sure you feel the same. At least, the cues you've been giving me would have meant just that when we were married."

She began a reply but changed her mind. He'd read the cues correctly, the ones she'd hoped she hadn't been sending.

"Can you deny you have feelings for me? Because I sure as hell have some urges I'd like to act upon." He swigged the last of his wine. "And right now, they're more than friendly."

Jack placed the empty glass carefully before him. "The main problem I have is understanding how to be friends with you. We don't know much about each other. I'm not so sure the type of relationship friends build is possible with us."

She kept her head down to hide the tears gathering at the backs of her eyes. Here's where he blew her off, right after she'd realized—

He lifted her chin with one finger. "You may not believe this, but I haven't always gotten everything I've wanted." He sighed. "On the surface, yes. I've been lucky. Born with a talent and allowed to share it with the world. Money, prestige, and yes, beautiful women." He looked out the window then back at her.

"I can't deny that never mattered." Jack leaned forward. "Those experiences brought me here, now. I can't rewrite the past but I can create a future. With Carlos and Abby." He laid his palm over her hand. "And, I hope with you. Friends or more, it's up to you."

She attempted to swallow past the sandpaper lining her throat. "W-what do you mean?"

"You know. I can see it in your eyes. I've spent years trying to forget you. That will never happen." He grasped her hand, lacing their fingers together. "I've thought about us, our mistakes, what we got right in the past several days. Let's work our way back to trust. Or actually, find the trust we never had."

She took a deep breath. Holy hello. She'd had way too much to drink. No way she'd heard correctly.

"If love can't exist between us, spending time together may help us become the friends Carlos wants us to be." His voice deepened. "I'm not the prodigal divorced husband, and I don't want a fatted tofu calf, only an opportunity to figure out what's up. Not for Carlos. For us."

She smiled. She'd always loved his sense of humor. When they'd faced difficult times, their laughter had held them together, until finally laughter hadn't been enough. "I think, I mean I believe you're right. I can't deny the attraction." She tapped her lips with her finger. "Let's start with being friends."

His troubled expression cleared. "Okay. I can work with that, yeah. Friends talk on the phone, right? They text? So I'll call from Arizona, we'll talk. And plan get-togethers like tonight. Friends do stuff together. I'd like you to see my cottage." He placed his other hand over both of theirs. "I'll make sure you don't regret giving me time."

Sally's thoughts wobbled like a bicycle wheel with missing spokes. Dang it, Jack had pulled her into his vortex again. Maybe this really was all about Jack and she'd misread him. Wouldn't be the first time she'd erred. Her heart told her he meant his words, but she'd followed her heart before, right up to a bad ending. Now her brain suggested playing it safe. Maybe this time she should listen to her head.

Her chest hurt. Ignoring her heart wouldn't work. She'd give him the time they both needed then wait to see what happened next.

Chapter Eight

"You know what? It doesn't matter." Sally slapped her hand over her mouth. She hadn't meant to speak her thoughts.

"What doesn't matter, Sally?" Abby leaned forward on the store's couch. "Do you mean you aren't upset that Carlos is traveling with his father? Or will you try telling me your thoughts were somewhere else." She smiled. "I've been practicing reading auras, and yours is bright and clear."

"I've created a monster."

Abby blew on her fingernails and polished them against her jersey top. "Yeah, great huh?"

Sally tapped her fingers on her chair arm, glad she could see Abby's bright halo again. "Speaking of auras, yours has changed recently. Sure you don't have some news?"

"If you mean the wedding date, you'll have to wait until Carlos returns. I promised him I wouldn't reveal our state secret without him in attendance."

Sally clapped her hands and moved beside Abby to give her a hug. "Finally. I'm going to be a mother-in-law." She leaned back. "I know you two will have a long and happy life together. I couldn't be more pleased."

"So, your knowledge." Abby put air quotes around the last word. "Are you making that up, or do you know for sure?"

"No one knows anything for sure, and arguments happen. But I've known from the moment we met that you and my son were destined." She smiled. "And are grandbabies not far behind? You know that's my biggest desire."

Abby smiled and wagged her finger. "Nope. Not gonna catch me."

Sally relaxed, willing to let her son and Abby tell her in their own time. "Enough of you trying to worm secrets out of me. What news of Carlos's big trip? I know he calls or texts you every time he paddles around a new curve on the Colorado River."

"He doesn't." Abby blushed. "Well, only when he can get a signal."

"Yeah, and I've heard your phone pinging nonstop with new texts, which must be when they finally get through. I'm looking forward to the big photo download when they reach the hotel later this week."

"Me too. We'll finally be able to Skype." Abby grasped her elbows, a sign that she wanted to speak seriously. "You know, Sally, I haven't stuck my nose in, but I'm curious. How is Jack's presence affecting you? You look happy for Carlos, but aren't you the least bit upset? Jealous? Hurt or something? I would be all of those, in spades."

"Dang. I shouldn't have helped you move that ghost out of your house. Then I wouldn't have a know-it-all as a friend and neighbor."

"Do you really think I won't notice your subject change? Wimpy try, Sally, really below your standards."

She shook her head. "Right. Well, you know, Jack

is Carlos's business, not mine. We're trying to get along because our son asked. We're adults. We can handle the situation."

"Hmm, that tells me you still harbor some feelings for him. Yep, I knew it. Your big, showy 'let me help you pack, son' comments are a bunch of hooey. You've kept your eagle eye on the two of them since Jack showed up."

Carlos's welfare had determined Sally's guidelines for interactions with her former spouse. While Jack had been true to his word and made "friendly" calls and sent texts before and during his Grand Canyon trip, she'd reserved judgment on his motives. Neither of them had mentioned their conversations to Carlos, and she hadn't decided why they kept their overtures toward each other a secret.

"Yes, well, I can't help wanting to ensure Carlos doesn't get hurt." She held up her hand, palm out. "I know. I can't protect him, but he's still my baby. You'll know what I mean when you have children. And will that be soon?"

"Not answering and I'd like to remind you that you pushed my buttons and made me face my fears not long ago. It's time I returned that favor. Tell me, what the heck happened to your marriage? Jack seems like a nice guy, you're fabulous, and I remember you telling me that your marriage was a failed dream. Why?"

Abby was right to push, but it sure didn't feel good. Her future daughter-in-law deserved the truth. The story could help in her marriage.

"We didn't trust our love," she said. "If we had, there's no way we could have been tricked by his father, grandfather, and a firm of underhanded attorneys. We sure as heck wouldn't have divorced without talking it out first."

"You were young and foolish, right?" Abby chewed her lip, her forehead creased. "How old were you, anyway?"

"We were both eighteen when we met at Woodstock, twenty-four when we divorced. We had more dreams than sense or money." She crossed her legs and smoothed down her skirt, buying herself time to avoid Abby's questions, or rather, facing her own answers.

Abby tapped Sally's arm. "Now you have the sense and he has the money. And you've both made dreams come true for yourselves. You should get together and try again."

Sally threw her an exasperated look. "I don't think so."

"Okay, I won't push you. Even though it's obvious...never mind." Abby shifted in her chair. "Have you decided about the Charlotte concert?"

"No, um, no. I'm not sure Jack really wants me there. I think he offered as a courtesy." That was a lie. He'd made it clear that he wanted her there. But she'd have to face old friends, the rest of the Rough Cuts, along with Mitch. Not a pleasant thought.

Abby pulled her phone out of her bag and began tapping out a text. "Sorry, I have to get this message. Business."

She hadn't heard a phone ring. Abby must have been attuned to the alert.

Her friend shoved the phone back into her bag and swiped her palms together. "Done deal."

She didn't like the satisfied gleam surrounding

Abby. "What do you mean? That text wasn't about business, unless it was funny business. What have you done?"

Abby examined her fingers. "You made me face my fears, now it's your turn."

"What. Did. You. Do?" She was pleased to note her tone sounded clipped, not upset.

"Don't flip out. You can handle this."

"Tell me."

"Carlos has received a text saying you'll be attending the Charlotte gig." Abby stood. "No more games, Sally. Heal or not, up to you. But Carlos and I won't stand by and watch regret cut you up into slivers. The grandchildren you crave deserve emotionally whole grandparents."

Abby was right, and she'd needed a push. "Fine thing, trying to manipulate me with grandchildren. Shame on you."

Abby shrugged. "Hey, we learned from the best, remember?"

As they stood at the doorway to Good Vibes, she voiced a nagging question. "You didn't type very much. How will Carlos understand your message?"

She smirked. "Thinking you'll get out of the trip with us? No way. We agreed on a catch phrase before he left."

Sally raised her eyebrows. "And?"

"The die is cast."

Great. They'd chosen the words attributed to Julius Caesar before his actions began a civil war.

"Fine. You've left me no option but to gird my loins and cross the Rubicon."

"I know."

Chapter Nine

Days later, Sally looked up when her store bell rang. "Carlos! I'm glad you're back."

"Me, too."

She scolded herself for feeling relief that his trip might not have been perfect. Glee replaced her shame. "What happened? Abby said you were enjoying yourself."

"I did. Jack was a great companion. He made sure our accommodations were top notch, and with kids back in school, the crowds weren't too heavy."

"Oh, I see. Silly me. You missed Abby, of course."

"Angling for a compliment, Mom?" He pulled her into a hug. "Yes, I missed you, too. Traveling first class is a blast, but my two favorite women weren't there to make the experience perfect."

She pulled away with a light swat at his chest. "Don't worry. I didn't replace you while you were gone. You're still my favorite son."

"Good to know, favorite mom."

"Would you like dinner at my house tonight, or are you too tired?"

"That's why I stopped by. Abby finished her commission and we're celebrating. Come over at six for drinks."

"I'm glad you two finally combined households. I like having you next door."

"You can stop worrying. Abby takes good care of me."

She shook her head. "You're joking, right? Did you learn nothing during those years teaching psych? Mothers cornered the market on worrying centuries ago." She patted his cheek. "I hope Abby will discover that fact for herself one day, soon."

"Yeah, well, first things first. You promise you'll come for dinner?"

She sensed his excitement. "Should I bring champagne? Dessert?"

"No, we have everything under control. Six o'clock. Don't be late."

"I'll be there."

"Good." He hugged her again and headed for the door. His hand on the doorknob, he turned. "By the way, Jack will be there, too." Carlos wrenched open the door and hurried out, throwing final words over his shoulder. "See you at six."

The door fell shut. Sally's jaw remained dropped. Her son had become devious over the years, and she had only herself to blame.

While she felt more comfortable with Jack after their conversations, she hadn't seen him since their dinner at Celeste's. When he'd laid a goodnight kiss on her that made her shiver remembering it, she'd told herself the wine was to blame, even though she'd stopped drinking in preparation to drive. Wasn't her fault her bones melted. That had been a side effect of Jack's magnetism. He'd always had that effect, and now that she understood her susceptibility, she'd make sure not to get caught again.

But oh, she couldn't deny the thought left her

feeling empty.

\*\*\*\*

Jack pulled up to the curb and turned off the car. He eyed the bouquet he'd picked up in Stratton. He should have gone with a smaller bunch. The damn thing all but took up the entire passenger seat. He'd had to seat belt the vase in to keep it standing upright. He hoped Abby wouldn't think he tried to buy her off. He had so many years to make up for, and some emotions he still found difficult to voice.

He adjusted his ball cap and sunglasses then eased out of the car. Wrestling with the flower arrangement, he headed for the front door, more nervous than expected. Although he and Carlos had made significant inroads on their trip together, this was his first visit to his son and Abby's home.

As he started up the drive, he noticed Sally exiting her front door. She didn't seem to notice him. Unless he slowed down, they'd arrive together. He maintained his pace.

They met at the bottom of the stairs.

"Sally."

"Jack."

"After you."

She nodded.

Shit. Why did he even bother calling her? She seemed determined to keep him at arm's length. Her friendly attitude during their regular conversations drove him crazy. She'd finally agreed to another dinner after turning down a meal before the Arizona trip.

Would building trust always be so difficult? Was it even possible?

Her hand trembled when she gripped the railing.

That's why he kept trying. Because whenever he lost hope that they'd ever move past the friend stage, some small tell would let him know she wasn't as calm as she appeared. He merely needed patience and a chance to kiss her again. He knew he'd pressed her buttons when he'd last laid one on her.

Feeling better, he whistled under his breath and followed her to the door. He shifted the flowers to one arm and with Sally, simultaneously raised a fist to knock. They exchanged glances and smiles as Abby appeared in the entrance. The dogs, Bunny and Henry, slid to a stop against Abby's legs.

"Welcome. Glad you both could make it."

Her emphasis on the word "both" left no doubt as to what Carlos and Abby desired.

"Oh, I love the flowers. They are for me, right?"

Yep, no flies grew on her. "They are." He hefted the vase and passed it to her.

"I've got the perfect place for these." She held the door open with her hip. "Come in. Carlos is checking the oven. He'll be right out."

The dogs demanded attention until Carlos appeared. Then they turned and led the way into the living room. Jack settled across from the fireplace, the dogs at his feet. A small fire burned. Sally disappeared into another room, presumably the kitchen.

"Nice home you've created."

"It's Abby's, well, now ours," Carlos said. "You should have seen it before she worked her magic. What a wreck." He rested one ankle on his knee. "Did most of the work herself. The paintings in here are hers, too. Wait until you see what she's done with the kitchen. She's amazing."

"Yeah, I think you mentioned that once or oh, about one hundred times. Every day we were away." He studied the artwork. "Strong lines, good use of color. I get why you brag."

Carlos grinned. "Bad habit, I guess."

"Nah, I'm glad you found your special woman. Don't let her go, son."

He shook his head. "I waited too long to find her. She's not getting away."

"Who's not getting away?" Abby strode in carrying a platter of hors d'oeuvres. She set the plate on the table and bent to kiss Carlos. Henry sat politely off to the side, waiting for people error. "You'd better be talking about me."

Carlos pulled her down beside him on the couch. "You bet I am. Don't even think about leaving. Well, except for putting dinner on the table. I'm okay with that."

"You'd better be, because you're helping."

"You're in command."

Jack wasn't blind to the heat between them. Yep, his son had the moves, and the right woman. Now it was time for the old man to score. He'd wanted to come to terms with Sally so he could move on and look for a new woman. He rubbed his jaw. Since they began talking again, he'd been deluged with memories of the good times. The physical attraction hadn't disappeared, either, though he wasn't sure she felt the magnetism as much as he did. Could be he hadn't thought his future plans through. Could be Sally was his answer.

Time would tell.

\*\*\*\*

Sally took a deep breath trying to calm her nerves,

but the extra oxygen didn't help. The glasses on the drink tray she held rattled. She returned the tray to the kitchen counter and sipped wine, concentrating on steadying her emotions. Henry had followed Abby and the food tray to the living room, but Bunny sat at her feet in silent support.

"Bunny, I hadn't expected to meet Jack at the door."

The small apricot-colored poodle mix tilted her head. Her liquid brown eyes seemed to understand Sally's words.

"You get it, don't you, sweet pup? We almost looked like a couple walking in together." She took a deep breath. "So what if we've had dinner together and talk on the phone. We're not a couple. Can't be. Crap. I never should have agreed to dinner at his house tomorrow night."

Bunny moved closer, sitting on Sally's shoe.

"I gotta tell you, cutie pie, I don't like this family night stuff. Carlos may get his hopes up, and then what?"

The dog sneezed then shook out her fur.

"You're right. It's not *his* hopes that may be destroyed. I'm lying. Again. Thanks for listening."

She grabbed the tray, pasted a smile to her face, and sailed out with Bunny to join the others. "Here we go. White wine and beer coming right up." She set the tray on the table rather than serving each person, not wanting to stretch her nerves any further.

She claimed an overstuffed chair sited as far from Jack as possible. Making nice for dinner was one thing, sitting close to him under the regard of discerning eyes another. "Here's to Abby's completed job," she said.

After exchanging the toasts, silence fell.

Carlos and Abby exchanged glances. Abby nodded and he cleared his throat.

"Celebrating Abby's job isn't the real reason we asked you here. Well, it is, but we have another aim for having you to dinner." Carlos looked between Jack and Sally. "We'd promised we'd tell you first, so that's why you're both here."

He placed his beer on the table.

The wedding date? Finally. "So? We aren't getting any younger," Sally said.

"Spit it out," Jack said at the same time.

"Abby finally agreed to set a date."

Abby blushed. "He makes it sound as if I was dragging my feet. We only met in June."

Jack and Sally spoke together. "You know when it's right." Jack glanced at her. She looked away from him and toward Abby.

"I'm excited for you," she said. "What date did you choose? Soon, but not too soon, I hope. Plans. We have to make plans."

Carlos held up his hand like a traffic cop. "Before you go all Momzilla on me, you need to hear what we'd like from you." He looked to Jack. "You, too."

Her heart stuttered. She had a bad feeling.

"The wedding will be private. Abby, me and immediate family. This is our ceremony, and we don't want a circus." He put his arm around Abby, pulling her close. "That said we want you two to stand up for us. We want you at our sides, not watching from a distance." The couple exchanged glances. "It would mean the world to us if you'd both agree."

*Dear Goddess. Could tonight hold any more*

*emotional hits?* Sally smoothed away tears, took a deep breath and spoke, her voice high and reedy to her ears. "You bet I'll be your witness." She stood and moved to the couch, her need to hug the couple overwhelming. "Thank you for asking."

Jack had stood with her. "I can't tell you how much this means to me." His voice had broken on the last words.

She reached for her wine and gulped. She'd been trying to keep an emotional distance from Jack so they'd have the opportunity to become friends. Otherwise, they'd jump into bed as they had when they met. And the future would replicate the past. If Carlos and Abby knew about the on-going contact between her and Jack, their curiosity would have no bounds. Now they'd be thrown together on a regular basis. Ai-yi-yi.

Sally watched the scene unfold like a well-known movie. She'd seen this coming for months, but the reality eluded her. Why were Carlos and Abby suddenly making a move? Was she pregnant? Abby swallowed her wine. Nope, not pregnant.

Abby caught her eye then twined her arm through Sally's, drawing her to the side. "We'll hold the ceremony here. This is our refuge, so it makes sense to us. Plus we want the dogs to participate."

"I get that." She cleared her throat. "What's the date? I'll need to circle it in red on my calendar."

"Thanksgiving weekend. Coffee house business is slow, I don't have any jobs planned, and Jack will be off tour."

"But that's...that's only two months away. Are you sure? Not that I'm complaining, and I guess if you aren't having a reception, the short time period is workable."

"Of course we're having a reception," Abby said.

Carlos interrupted his low-voiced conversation with Jack. "We talked about holding it at the coffee house, but we figured that space wouldn't be big enough, so we reserved the Blue Peak Inn."

"The Inn." Sally's knees weakened. "Nice." And romantic. "Lucky you were able to reserve it at this late date."

"Everything fell into place." Abby hugged her. "You always say, if your plans fall into place easily, your wish or desire is meant to be."

"Right, that's right." She raised her glass and noticed it was empty. Criminy. She'd be drunk in no time if she kept slamming down drinks. "So, what can I do to help?"

"I've got a list," Abby said. Her soon-to-be daughter had list making down, or rather up to, an elevated art. Even a resident ghost hiding her to-do log hadn't slowed her down or prevented Abby from making her dreams come true.

"Not surprised."

"I'm hoping you'll help me with one other thing— kind of a big thing, I guess."

She swallowed. What could be harder than standing across from Jack while watching their son marry? She shouldn't have asked. She knew how the universe acted. Ask and you get, and not always in the form you expected.

"Um, well, sure, I guess. What do you need?"

Abby swigged her drink. "My mother will want to take over. Make this into the sort of wedding she thinks I should have."

"You were pretty clear about your wishes with us just now."

Abby put down her glass and clasped her elbows. "Yeah, but you don't know her. I'm stronger thanks to you, and you'd think I could stand up for myself at thirty-five years old, but I swear Mom's a force of nature." She shook her head. "No, you're the force of nature. My mom is…a force of a different kind. Not like *Encounters of the Third Kind*, but in a strange way, close to that. If I hadn't seen my birth certificate, I'd swear I'd been podded."

They'd had discussions about Abby's mother, and Sally was well aware of the hurting that woman had put on her daughter. She'd try to hold her tongue, but if an opportunity arose to set the woman straight, she wouldn't remain quiet.

Oh, hell. Not only would she have the stress of standing up with Jack, she'd have to play nice with a stranger she already disliked. Could be worse. At least she wouldn't have to dance with Jack. She tuned back in to Abby.

"And we've got a great band. We're hoping you'll do the whole first dance thing with us. You know, wedding couple with their parents?"

Surprise, surprise. And the universe scored again.

****

Jack had been sure he knew what was coming tonight, but he'd been only partly correct. He'd overheard enough on the Grand Canyon trip to know Carlos and Abby were setting a wedding date. Only the advance information hadn't alerted him to his part in their special day. He'd been blind-sided, but in a great way. Given the expression on Sally's face, she hadn't expected their announcement, either.

He glanced at her as she chatted with Abby in front of the fireplace. The flames and lamplight combined to add highlights to Sally's hair and soften her appearance. She looked the way he remembered her, young, vibrant, and open.

Maybe not so open right now. That frown didn't bode well for his need to know if what was happening between them was closure or an opening to a whole new world. Think positive, man. Her frown could be caused by someone or something else.

He thought back to their dinner at Celeste's. She'd kissed him goodnight in the parking lot, and then jumped into her car as if he had a communicable disease. That kiss had given him hope, though. Because if that defined the type of kiss she gave her friends these days, he wouldn't survive one night as her lover. One night hell—one hour. The heat, and the hard-on, had made the short drive home memorable and uncomfortable.

He knew from Carlos's raised tone that he'd asked a question, but Jack had no clue about the inquiry.

"Sorry. What did you ask?"

"Checking Mom out, huh? She still looks great, right?" He rushed on without waiting for an answer. "What I said was, we've hired a local band for the reception. Not on the Rough Cuts level, but good, really good. Mostly cover songs, some originals. They do well around here, and we were lucky to get them. Anyway, Abby has her heart set on the whole first dance thing."

"That's nice, yeah. A good memory for you. Go for it."

"You don't get it. The parents dance the first

number, too. They join in later. So I asked if that would bother you. A slow dance with Mom."

Sally turned his way. She looked appalled, or possibly scared.

Abby punched the air with her fist. "She said yes. The first dance is on!"

"I guess that's your answer." Carlos grinned. "Abby and Mom are so much alike sometimes it's scary. Together they can rock worlds."

He already knew Sally could rock his world for both good and bad. Unfortunately, if her frown gave any indication, he was more like to get stoned—in the biblical sense—not rocked.

Chapter Ten

Jack opened his door to Sally. His thoughts froze on "Wow." He swallowed his spit. He'd thought the black dress Sally had worn the last time was hot. The green suit she had on tonight kicked his ass. Could be she'd worn the suit to keep things from heating up, but that wouldn't fly. She couldn't know the professor look turned him on. Yeah, he was one twisted bastard.

"Come on in. You have any problem finding the place?"

"No. I like driving around the lake, checking out the colors during autumn. I knew how to find your neighborhood, though I'd never passed through the gates."

Jack handed her a glass of wine and offered hors d' oeuvres.

"Great pâté," she said. "Did Pete cater tonight?"

The corners of his mouth turned up. "I do cook, remember?" He leaned closer and snagged a canapé. Her heat and scent filled his senses. His head spun. "I hope you like the wine."

"Right, yes, the wine is…lively. Fresh, fruity with undertones of herbs and, is that vanilla?" She tilted her head. "Nice finish."

"Good." Deep silence gathered between them. Having Sally in his home sped from good idea to an open pit of danger. A secret, one she may not believe as truth, lay down the hall.

She gulped her wine, setting the empty glass on the cocktail table and folding her hands together. He half expected her to cross her legs at her ankles and balance a book on her head.

"Your house is lovely. This was your uncle's home? I'm sorry I never got to meet him. How long have you lived here?"

Her voice was high and she raced through her speech. Nice to know they shared something, though nerves wasn't his first pick for mutuality.

"I've been coming here since I was a kid, starting with short summer vacations. I inherited a few years ago, but until recently I only spent a few weeks a year here."

"But this room has such a warm feel. Lived in and cared for. Comfortable, yet stylish."

She liked his home. Score one in his campaign to win her over. "I did some remodeling, added on a room. Would you like a quick tour?"

Oh, shit. His mouth operated independently. Still, the door to the past had been opened weeks ago, and not by him. Time to show her another part of his life and hope for the best.

"That'd be nice, yes," she said. "Thanks."

They slipped out of the room and down a short hallway to the foyer. He led her through the house, gauging her reaction to the heart pine wood paneling, stone fireplace, vaulted ceiling and original Arts and Crafts furniture. The more she praised, the looser his muscles became.

He stopped at a closed door. His nerves kicked up to staccato. "This is my favorite room." He threw open the door and stepped back.

Sally threw him a questioning glance. "Better not be your bedroom." She stepped inside. He followed, seeing the familiar room with new eyes, hoping he hadn't made a mistake sharing with her.

One wall made mostly of glass overlooked a view of the lake and surrounding trees. A French door to the side led onto a small deck that boasted two deck chairs. Guitars on stands were stationed around the room. His framed music awards covered almost two walls. Would she think his display arrogant?

Her complete stillness told him she'd noticed the baby grand situated in front of the windows.

She pointed then dropped her hand, but not before he'd noticed her shaking fingers. "Are those—?"

He cleared his throat, but his reply sounded husky. "Yeah." The photographs she'd left behind when she'd run from him were arranged on his piano, still in the original cheap plastic frames she'd bought.

"How did you?" Her shoulders hunched.

"Our flaky neighbor saw the box at the curb. She saved the photos. She was sure I'd be looking for you and Carlos." He put his hands on her shoulders, feeling her shaking abate. "I packed some of the stuff away for a while to keep our secret, but I never threw out anything important from our time together."

She exhaled. "I don't know what to say."

"You don't have to say anything." Tears pooling in her eyes convinced him he hadn't made a mistake in bringing her here. He'd been afraid she'd think he hauled out the photos to make points with her, but her reaction told him differently. Taking a chance when they met again, revealing he'd searched for her, had been his only indication to her until now. Photos did speak.

Her eyes glistened. "I never knew," she whispered.

Their gazes tangled. A sense of yearning, of wanting more, swept him. So close, and now, more open to him than she'd been so far. He placed his palm on the side of her face brushing a tress of soft hair from her forehead.

"This is a dream. Has to be." She licked her lips.

"No dream, babe. This is real. You. Me. Us."

His gaze locked on her glistening mouth. "Together again. I'd add naturally, but that's not true, is it? We've had to fight to get to this point. And damned if I know where we're going."

"I think we're headed in well, maybe not the right direction, but at least we've shifted."

"So I can kiss you now?"

She nodded. "That'd be nice."

*"Nice" hell. This chance had to count big.* He bent closer, his lips skimming hers in first contact. He angled for more.

The house phone rang, shattering their intimacy. Shit. Talk about bad timing.

She edged from him, hugging her elbows like a waif in one of those late-night charity commercials. For the first time he could remember, she looked ravaged.

"Guess you'd better answer, huh."

He checked caller ID. Mitch. "Damn it." He snatched up the phone. "This had better be good."

"I think it is," Mitch said. "I've got the rehearsal space. Be there in three days. I'll e-mail the information tomorrow."

He tempered his tone and watched Sally move to

the piano and pick up a picture frame "So why'd you call?"

"So you couldn't say you didn't know when to show. Three days, Jack. No excuses."

"Fine. I hear you."

Ending the call, he joined Sally. He slipped his arms around her waist, marveling at the curves that still sparked a physical reaction.

"I remember the day you took this," she said. "We were picnicking at the arboretum. PB&J sandwiches and lemonade."

"Frisbees. Was that the day the kite broke free?"

She smiled. "No, that was…in April. This was July. See the sparkler package in the basket?"

"Carlos loved those damn things, didn't he? And those charcoal snakes your dad gave him." He turned her in his arms, the material of her suit sliding under his hands.

"Yeah, he still buys bargain-sized packs of each every summer." Her smile slipped. "I'm so sorry, Jack. You missed so much. I—"

He rested his fingers over her lips. "Stop. We both screwed up. Let's kick our regrets in the ass."

Removing his fingers from her lips, he finally claimed the taste he'd wanted but not admitted since his first glance outside her store. Sweet as the kiss was, he still wondered. Would they ever overcome their past? His thoughts slipped away as passion claimed his attention.

****

Jack entered the rehearsal space they'd booked in Atlanta. Most of the band lived on the East coast or in the Midwest. Besides a central location and major airport, the tour opened here. His buddies waited for him, along with Mitch.

Mitch rubbed his hands together. "Right, you're all here. I've got some good news. You know the dates sold out in hours, right?"

Jack's stomach churned. He hoped Mitch hadn't added shows at the end of the tour. No way he'd miss Carlos and Abby's wedding. Plus, he couldn't come to terms with Sally—whatever those were—when he was on the road.

"I negotiated top money and added another show when I could. We had extra travel days built in, so the new dates worked. Extra money, no extra travel."

Jack felt his anger slip rein. "Extra work, Mitch. You didn't mention that."

"I built in down time with the promoters."

"You shoulda asked first."

Mitch rubbed his hand over his wiry hair. "Have you checked your messages? I called. Everyone else is cool with the added dates. Besides, the second shows are already sell outs."

Jack studied the floor. "Okay, then." He looked each of his long-time friends in the eye in turn. "I'm telling you now, though, I won't tour again." He paused. "This is my last go round."

Everyone froze. "I'll make albums with you as long as Mitch gets us contracts and you want me. But no more tours."

"Shit, I wish I'd known that." Mitch scratched his head. "We coulda added more cities."

Jack glared at their manager.

Mitch held up his hands, palms out. "Just kidding, Jack. We all heard you making noise about not touring, but we thought you'd get restless and want to go out again."

He shook his head. "Nope. I'm done. I know what I want and it's not what I've had. You all have families. My son is getting married at Thanksgiving. You know what I'm saying."

Mitch said, "Shit, man, the media is gonna eat this up."

He shook his head. "Not a word. I don't want the info about this being my last tour leaked. After the tour is over, fine. But not before. Or during. And don't even consider mentioning Carlos's identity or wedding. Agreed?"

Jack heard variations of "We'll keep it quiet." A niggling fear hit his spine but he tamped it down.

"Look, I know we'd have gotten more money with a last tour billing, but I can't spend what I've already got, can you?"

His friends grinned and shook their heads.

"Hell," Tony said. "We'll have more fun this way, putting something over on the press for a change."

Jack picked up his guitar. "You said it. Let's kick ass."

\*\*\*\*

Sally had thought she'd breathe easier with Jack in Atlanta. She'd hoped that planning a wedding with Abby would distract her. Help her forget. The opposite occurred.

The looming wedding dance with Jack took position front and center in her thoughts. How could having his arms and unique scent surrounding her again, even in public, be a smart idea?

Their recent shared kisses had about sent her into

the stratosphere. She'd decided a kiss—or two—would immunize her to his presence. What had she been thinking? Talk about stupid moves. The way he'd responded had ignited a fire that still burned. Neither of them had mentioned the kisses, and she wouldn't. She couldn't, even if she'd like to know if her reaction to him had been more a blast to the past than anything. Especially after she'd seen their old family photos on his piano.

Dang Carlos and Abby. Why had she agreed to the dance? Not that she had. Abby had taken her inability to speak as a positive answer. Of course, the tradition was for the parents to exchange partners, so she could do the pretty then move on to Abby's father.

Her one satisfaction came from knowing Abby's parents had less a wish to dance together than she did with Jack. Abby said their acrimonious parting had made the top ten list of all-time worst divorces.

Her thoughts turned to the Stephens family. Abby had warned Sally, but the reality proved worse. Abby's mother had attempted to disrupt the wedding plans during the announcement call Abby had made using a speakerphone. She hadn't even asked to meet Carlos, instead mentioning her daughter's poor choice of partner, apparently based solely on, what? His name? The woman was a professional menace.

Her heart pounded, her blood pressure spiked given the flush that covered her arms and prickled her neck. She'd promised Abby she'd help keep their plans on track, but her mother-in-law counterpart made academic power plays look like grade school playground bullying. So far Abby had found ways to either compromise or stand firm, but the stress showed in her face.

As if conjured, Abby entered Good Vibes. The metal bell above the door clanged wildly. Abby's aura showed jagged streaks of angry red.

"Whoa, Abby. Let me make you some chamomile tea. Your aura hit the shop before you did."

The young woman's frown smoothed. She slumped, as if in relief. "Thanks, Sally. Oh, and good afternoon. I apologize for busting in, but I've been abused via phone."

"Then you need a hug. Come here."

"I'm feeling better, thanks." Abby inhaled. "You and your store always calm me." She placed her hand on Sally's arm. "So does being with you. I get to believing that all things are possible with you and Carlos on my side."

"I'm glad, but remember that your strength is your own. But, because today is sunny, I'll take your compliment and raise you one. That blue top you're wearing enhances your eye color and shows off your curves. I'm glad you deep-sixed the over-alls and work boots."

Abby shook her head and eyed Sally's loose tie-dyed cotton top, dangling jewelry and black leggings. "We've had this discussion before. Our idea of styling will never match. Not in this lifetime or any number of the others we've shared. Which I don't remember but I take your word for our long history." She leaned closer. "Fashion is a dictate. You're the real deal."

Sally's throat held a lump. She swallowed several times. "Still want that tea?"

"Thanks, but don't bother. I'm headed across the street. Want to join me?"

She put a "Back in ten minutes" sign on the door and they walked in to The Collective Unconscious Café. She enjoyed watching her son and his fiancée together, but never as much as when they spotted each other across a crowded room.

The two women settled at a table with coffee and fresh-baked scones. Good thing she'd passed on her good cook genes to Carlos. Abby had dropped weight and couldn't afford the loss. She watched Abby gather her thoughts.

"You won't believe what mother suggested now."

"Try me."

"She wants us to lock the dogs away during the ceremony. She thinks Henry and Bunny will bite someone."

Sally's jaw dropped. She studied her scone to hide her upset. "I thought—"

Abby nodded. "Yes. Henry is carrying my ring, and Bunny will handle Carlos's." She grinned. "You should see the two of them when we practice. They're rocking the assignment."

She hesitated. "So your mother has come to terms with a private wedding at the house?" Her forehead wrinkled. "Wasn't she lobbying for a ceremony at The Blue Peak Inn with a reception to follow immediately?"

"That was yesterday. Or the day before. Now she says she understands we want a private ceremony, but she thinks having the dogs participate will create a disruptive atmosphere rather than the decorous one a wedding demands."

Sally didn't need air quotes to know who'd said what. She struggled to keep her dismay and anger from showing. "You know I'll follow your wishes. I'm happy to be part of your special day."

Abby sighed. "I'm beginning to think we should have held the wedding and told her after it was a done deal."

"That option is still open," Sally said. "The ceremony is yours."

She grinned. "Don't think that idea hasn't crossed my mind." She munched a bite of scone, her forehead wrinkled in thought. "I have to make this stand. Even though mother lives a thousand miles away, she's still my parent. It's time I came to terms with all that means, both past and present."

Sally grasped Abby's hand. "I'm so proud of you."

"That makes two of us." Carlos pulled out a chair and settled beside Abby, his arm across her shoulders. He kissed her cheek.

She swallowed hard. Had she and Jack exchanged the same loving looks and touches? She knew they had, but memories of arguments and betrayal presided, even after learning the truth about their past.

"How can I help?"

"Listening is good," Carlos said.

Abby nodded. "I may need you to run interference once she arrives."

"Arrives?" Sally caught her breath. "You don't mean—when is she coming? Exactly?"

The couple's glum looks answered her question before Carlos spoke. "Too soon."

Abby placed her hand atop Sally's. "Would you mind keeping her busy?"

"You mean out of your sight? Sure, I can take her to Asheville. Lots of cute shops will keep her busy. Or is she an outdoors girl? Plenty of places to hike around here."

"Better take her to the nicest places in Asheville. You know, the boutiques and galleries. Add a linen tablecloth restaurant with an extensive wine list for lunch and you'll have a friend for life." Abby bit her lower lip. "That's pushing it. She'll be softened up, though."

"Gosh, and here I'd thought we could sit in on Asheville's Friday night drum circle downtown." She lightly chucked Abby's jaw. "Better close your mouth, sweetie. I know the right places to take your mother. She won't know she's been played."

Abby gave a weak grin. "I knew I could count on you."

Carlos leaned forward. "Simply because Abby wants help doesn't give you permission to set her mom straight." He rubbed the nape of his neck. "I know you, remember? All we need is help showing my future in-law around."

"I won't say anything she can't handle."

"That's not what I—"

Abby placed her fingers over Carlos's lips. "Shush. Whatever happens is meant."

He kissed her fingers then shifted closer to her. "I knew I was in for trouble when you started reading the claptrap my mom pushed on you."

She snorted. "It's not claptrap, and you're stuck in outmoded science."

Sally laughed at their interplay, but also caught the look her son leveled at her. She wouldn't promise not to set Margaret Stephens straight, but she'd watch her words. Sometimes, though, the truth revealed itself without human help. And Abby's mother needed a good talking to. She wondered what had set Abby's mother on her path, and whether she could be diverted.

"Exactly when does Margaret arrive?"

Her son's lips twitched. "Halloween weekend."

"Well, that's…nice." She complimented herself on refraining from saying "appropriate," but Abby's grin told her that her thoughts had been read. "So, I'll give you the weekend, then take her to Asheville on Monday. We can head over to Cashiers and some of the other smaller towns, too, that week. Will that help?"

Abby sighed. "Yes, thanks. I wish I could have prevented her coming early, though. We'd hoped for one last quiet dinner with you and Jack before the tour. Plus, I hate that you're closing the store to help us out. If I didn't have a deadline, I'd man the register."

"Hush, girlfriend, soon to be daughter. I'll get Deirdre Collins to come in and cover the store. Not a problem." She tapped her forefinger against her teeth. "And you may as well get the family meet and greet over before Jack leaves, so keep your dinner plans."

Carlos stood. "Thanks, Mom. I've gotta get back to the kitchen."

Abby leaned across the table. "I really, really appreciate you taking on mother. For sightseeing, I mean."

Sally heard the underlying meaning. She placed her hand over Abby's. "Don't worry. I won't say anything that shouldn't be voiced. My main concern is getting you married to my son, and I won't let anything, or anyone, stand in the way of that happening."

"Thanks. Have I told you lately that you are my very favorite person in the world?"

She raised her eyebrows. "Don't you mean favorite

female person? My son is your favorite, right?" She frowned. "Because if he's not, you've got some explaining to do, young woman."

Abby grinned. "Don't tell Carlos, but sometimes I think I love you more. You know, because you helped me find myself." She lowered her voice. "But mostly because you gave birth to and raised the one man in the world for me. When we have kids, I hope you'll teach our munchkins about the real meaning of life."

Sally wiped away her stray tears. "For balance, you mean? Someone to show my grandkids that Elvis is King, not science as Carlos believes?"

She nodded. Her eyes lost their mirth. "I'm hoping you can work out a truce with Jack. Having him around has made such a difference to Carlos." She bit her lip. "You'll always be his anchor, but Jack is an extra he never expected. I hope I didn't hurt your feelings saying this."

"No, you didn't. Carlos is happier since you, and Jack, entered his life. What kind of nasty ass would I be if I couldn't share him with others?"

Abby nodded and sipped her coffee. "So, how's it going with that? Sharing Carlos with Jack, I mean?"

Her nonchalant tone didn't fool Sally. "You can answer that, you've seen us together."

"You mean those have been the only times you've seen Jack? Huh. I heard—"

Sally thought quickly to avoid lying. "He's been rehearsing for the tour almost since their trip out West ended." She concentrated on her coffee.

"So you mean if you had a chance you'd meet Jack even without our invitation?"

She refrained from blurting out the truth. "No,

that's not what I said and stop trying to push us together. We live in two very different worlds. What we had, if anything, is so far in the past, I need a microscope to find traces of what we were." She sipped her coffee to relax her tight throat. "I know we had the 'I'd like a man' discussion, but I wasn't referring to Jack then. The truth is—"

"Better not finish that statement, Sally. I'd hate to listen to another lie."

Her jaw dropped. "What?"

"I'm really glad you taught me to read auras, that's all. I know you're hiding something."

"I've created a monster."

"You've said so before. Once more I'll take your sentiment as a compliment."

They finished their coffee, and their conversation skirted personal topics, a relief to Sally. She wondered what Abby had sensed in her statement about not needing Jack to be happy. She'd lived without a serious relationship for so long, she didn't know how including someone else in her life would work. A man wasn't required for happiness, but she also knew the failure of her young marriage had marked her, and not positively. Jack's reappearance had stirred the pot, that murky vessel she'd rather had been left undisturbed.

"So you'll come?"

Abby's question came from the blue. "Sorry, I didn't catch that last."

"To dinner. The night my mother arrives."

"Absolutely. Meanwhile, I'll send up some prayers that her trip is delayed. Oops. I shouldn't have said that."

"Sure you should. You always suspect my secret

desires."

And now her soon-to-be-daughter-in-law could read Sally in return. She'd have to watch her thoughts. Every single minute. The universe listened way too closely for her comfort. Nope. It wasn't the listening but the delivering of wishes that came too fast and unexpectedly that tied her in knots.

She'd never been good with macramé.

Chapter Eleven

Jack sensed turmoil before Carlos and Abby's door closed behind him. The atmosphere resembled the split second of stillness before thunder and lightning combined to create a sound like no other. Sally and a woman who must be Abby's mother had faced off before the fireplace.

Abby broke the silence. "Mother, this is Jonathan Young. Margaret Stephens, Jonathan."

Jack flinched. Why had they chosen to hide his identity?

She continued the introduction. "Mother lives in St. Louis and came in early to help."

His musician's ear heard the stress on her last word. Even had Carlos not clued him in, he'd have to have been totally self-absorbed not to sense the tension in Abby's formal speech patterns. Her stiff posture.

"Carlos's father is a, um, consultant. That's the best way to describe your business, isn't it?"

Her forehead sported perspiration. Where was Carlos and why wasn't next to Abby? His son entered the room with a drink tray. Ah. This group needed alcohol, if he were any judge. Lots of alcohol.

"Yes, that's right, Abby. I consult with others who work toward making the world a better place. We invest in the future, you could say." Hell, no lies there. Music, all the creative arts, made life worth living.

Margaret Stephens curled her lip. "I see."

Abby placed her hand on his arm. "Mother is unhappy with some of my changes. She prefers that I use my full name of Abigail, not Abby."

Once again, he heard the faint stress on her last word and smiled. A family dynamic he understood too well. Poor Abby.

He slipped his arm around her shoulders. "Marge, your daughter makes me wish I was young again. I'd pick her in a heartbeat. Abby is special, don't you agree? I'm glad she and Carlos are making a life together. Can't wait to see my grandkids. And the dogs—where are Henry and Bunny?"

Abby grimaced so quickly he wondered if he'd imagined her expression. "They're in the yard. We were afraid they'd be underfoot."

"Underfoot? But they were fine the last time I was here."

Sally grabbed a wine glass from the tray. Her face was red, and she shot a glare at Margaret. Aha.

She held up her glass. "Let's toast, shall we?"

Christ, even Sally sounded formal. He didn't intend to spend his last evening before the tour playing a game for Abby's mother. Oh, hell, sure he would.

"Here's to Carlos and Abby. May your happiness never end, your disagreements be minor, and your home continue as a sanctuary from the evils of the world."

He drank the toast but wanted to laugh, instead. Trust Sally to tell that biddy off in a way she wouldn't catch. He glanced at Margaret. Huh, maybe she did get the dig, after all. And these two mothers were set to spend a few days together? Could be going out on tour would be convenient, after all.

"Jonathan, perhaps you misheard. My name is Margaret, not Marge." Her scorn was palpable. "I'd appreciate your attention to detail."

"Sorry, my hearing isn't as sharp these days." Well, that was true enough. "Right. So, when did you arrive?"

"This afternoon, no thanks to Asheville's rinky dink airport. Honestly, closing down because of a little fog."

Abby set her glass on the tray. "Didn't you say that all flights were delayed in Atlanta?" She straightened. "Mother, the local airport can't land flights that never take off. The fog had lifted by the time you arrived."

His estimation of his future daughter-in-law rose. Abby one, Marge zero.

The older woman huffed. "You'd think the weather could have cooperated. My suitcase had gotten soaked by the time those luggage handler sluggards unloaded the plane. Honestly, people in the South move so slowly I don't know how anything is ever accomplished."

She sipped her wine, either ignoring or not understanding the room's thunderous quiet. "Forgive me, Mr. Young, but you and Carlos don't look Hispanic."

The non sequitur caught him off guard.

"Pardon me?" He quaffed his beer to gain time.

"You gave your son a Spanish name. I assumed you were a foreigner."

He held the beer in his mouth until he could swallow without choking. "My son's name was chosen for sentimental reasons. I'm sure you understand." He placed his beer on a nearby table, removing the temptation of dousing her with the liquid. "I've had some business in St. Louis on occasion. Why don't we sit? I'd like to hear a little more about your hometown."

"It's not my hometown—" she sniffed "—but my husband's. Rather my former husband. I was raised in Chicago, the Lincoln Park area. Are you familiar with the city?" Her doubt as to his sophistication was obvious.

Jack remembered the city for a reason she couldn't understand. The Rough Cuts had played a blues festival. What a rush, sharing a stage with many of his musical heroes.

"I've seen a bit of the city, yes. Toured some of The Art Institute. Their Impressionist exhibit is world class." Sally had shared her love of Impressionist art with him, and he'd gone to that wing, first. He'd spent less than an hour there before he'd been spotted, and had always meant to return.

"Well, then you understand that Chicago has much to offer." She began a monologue on the pleasures of her hometown.

Jack made appropriate noises when she paused. The grins on everyone's face but hers told him the others enjoyed having a secret over Marge. But why perpetrate the hoax? And why disguise his true identity?

He saw his chance to push for answers when he followed Carlos to the kitchen. "Carlos, what the hell is going on out there? What kind of game are you playing?"

His son grinned. "You mean you haven't deduced that Abby's mother is difficult? She thinks Abby is 'marrying down,' whatever the hell that means."

"I figured out she's a stone cold bitch, yeah. I thought you were ashamed of me or something." Shit. Where had that come from?

Carlos lowered his voice. "No way. Abby is afraid her mother will spill the beans to the media. She's all about the spotlight, ya know. Her daughter marrying a celebrity's son is more in line with what she sees as her daughter's right." He ran his fingers through his hair. "We want a quiet wedding. Margaret wants the type of event that shows up in the social columns of the newspaper."

"So, why don't you and Abby change your wedding date, have the ceremony you want, and present it to the bitch as a done deal?"

"That's what mom suggested too." He rubbed the nape of his neck. "But Abby and I are decided. You and mom are standing up with us. Period. We want you with us, totally with us, not pulled away from your tour for the wedding. And we want it on the day we picked."

"Right. The day is astrologically auspicious, right?"

Carlos stared. "How did you know?"

"I knew your mother before you did, remember? And I've seen she and Abby together, heard their woo-woo speak."

"Yeah, they drive me crazy sometimes." He rubbed his neck. "I'm never gonna live down marrying a woman who shares mom's beliefs. But I don't care what day we get married as long as the deed is done, the sooner the better."

"Smart man."

"Besides, Grandmother Young has already made

plans. She's coming down the Monday before Thanksgiving. We'd really like her with us."

Carlos and Abby had spent a long weekend in Philadelphia, getting to know Jack's mother. He'd heard all about the visit from her, and hadn't recognized her new, enthusiastic approach to life. His son may never know what he'd set in motion by looking for his missing parent, but Jack understood. He did wonder what would happen when his mom and Sally met again all these years later. On second thought maybe not.

"So, what can I do to help?"

"Tonight? Go easy on Margaret, even though I know she could use a verbal slap to the ego. After that, go on tour and kick butt. I'm not driving to Charlotte to see an old, broken down man trying to regain his former glory with one last tour."

"Smart ass." He lightly cuffed his son on the shoulder. "I'll show you broken down."

\*\*\*\*

Sally wished she could scream. A primal and raw shriek. She figured that would be the only thing that could derail Margaret and give Abby a break.

She'd never regretted having a son, but had often wished she had a daughter to share girlie stuff with. Abby had quickly taken that place, as well as becoming a close friend. She cherished their relationship.

Not so, Margaret. If she wasn't haranguing Abby about the intimate wedding plans, attempting at every turn to reorganize the event to her own exacting standards, she was referring to Abby as Abigail. What part of change did this woman not understand?

Impressively, Abby kept her composure. What the heck kept Carlos? He needed to get his butt out here and support his fiancée.

Jack returned without Carlos. "Abby, Carlos needs your help getting the food out."

Abby's smile disappeared with her mother's next words.

"Carlos is the cook? Why am I not surprised," she said. "You never did like the domestic arts, Abigail."

Sally's hands clenched. "I've had wonderful meals with Abby as chef." The woman may not be attending her daughter's wedding. Instead, she'd be in traction somewhere far, far away. "And look around. The house is comfortable, welcoming. If those aren't domestic arts, then I'm not sure what you mean." She hugged Abby. Poor girl's shoulders were so stiff it felt like she wore football padding under her sweater.

"Homey? Displaying a smelly old pipe on the mantel? And who are those people in that photograph? Your relatives, I suppose." She sniffed. "They certainly aren't familiar to me."

Sally inhaled twice before answering. "The pipe came with the house and has sentimental value. And the couple portrayed is the Wilkinson's, the former owners. Lovely people."

"Who in the world would want that old stuff? Really, sometimes Abigail shows no artistic sense." Margaret's face wrinkles resembled a Shar Pei without the cute factor. "Besides, Carlos shouldn't be forced to help in the kitchen. That's women's work."

She'd heard this refrain often over her years teaching Women's Studies. Taking a deep breath, she reminded herself that everyone deserved an opinion. That didn't mean they had to air it or demand others fall in line with them.

"Carlos loves to cook. That's one reason his coffee house is popular. Plus, he and Abby are partners. In everything. The ideas about gender we grew up with aren't really…well, modern, are they?"

"Modern." Margaret sniffed. "I prefer tradition and substance."

She exchanged a look with Abby. "Hon, I think Carlos is waiting, and I'm hungry. Whatever you made for dinner smells great. Let's eat."

Abby grinned and left.

She tamped her anger. "I think Abby will impress you, Margaret, if you allow her room to grow. She is a talented, beautiful, and gracious woman, and I'm pleased she is joining our family."

Margaret sipped her wine. "That's nice. But don't you agree about this wedding?"

"I'm sorry?"

"Well, really. A private ceremony followed by a reception with, it sounds like, everyone in town invited. Not the exclusive event she should have. And she wants to include flea-bitten dogs. Honestly."

Sally moved to the edge of her seat. "Your daughter and my son have determined what they want for their wedding. Our role is to make this event special, not dictate what *we* want for *their* special day."

"Her first wedding was a shoddy affair, too. I'd so hoped she would have the wedding day of her dreams this time."

She refrained from mentioning that Abby had suggested the private ceremony, not Carlos. "Really? Abby hadn't confided those dreams."

Margaret smiled, a victorious gleam in her eye. "Well, yes. I often heard her mention her wish for a dress with a long train, lots of flowers, candles, soft music, her favorite people, you know, romantic and traditional."

She counted to three then sipped her drink, allowing her temper to continue cooling.

"Sounds like that's what Carlos and Abby have planned." Jack scratched his cheek with one slim finger. "Except the favorite people are limited to us. I'm feeling privileged."

She exchanged a quick glance with him. A small smile curved his lips.

"But what do I tell my friends? They felt slighted last time. And for Abigail to once again marry without inviting them? Well, I simply can't think how I'll face my bridge group."

"Mother, your friends are most welcome to attend our reception." Abby stood in the doorway, an oven mitt in her hand. "Let's not discuss this now. Tonight is our dinner for the families. We'd like you to learn more about each other."

Sally stood. "You are so right." She turned to Margaret. "Let's move on. By the way, have you heard the story behind the dining room's crystal chandelier?"

She was tempted to tell Margaret about the ghost who had inhabited this house, hoping it would send the shrew packing. Instead, she'd be good and stick to tedious, safe subjects. Damnation, sometimes being a loving parent stunk.

They sat at table, Sally and Jack to one side across from Margaret, with Carlos and Abby flanking them. To take her attention off the heat Jack threw—and her need to embrace it—she commented on the place settings. Abby glanced to her mother before answering.

"Yes, my grandmother had excellent taste."

"I'm glad you like the transferware, dear," Margaret said. Her jaw clenched as she picked up her knife and cut into her chicken.

"Mother prefers Waterford china." She smiled. "I'd rather eat off a plate I'm not afraid to touch. Or wash and dry."

Margaret opened her mouth, so Sally spoke first. "This is Wedgwood, isn't it? I'm not sure of the pattern name."

Everyone stared at her.

"What, did you think my interests are limited to, um, my store and my former profession? I happen to know that transferware became popular about 1750, and the industry was centered mainly in one area of England."

Jack grinned. "Are you about to go all professor on us, or can anyone join in?"

"By all means, join in." She mumbled, "If you can."

He leaned back in his chair. "What, did you think my interests are limited to, um, working to further the creative arts?"

*Smart butt.* "I had no idea you were interested in ceramics."

He eyed her. "You might be surprised to hear all my interests."

Their glances tangled and held. Sally's breath caught. He couldn't mean what his expression implied, could he? She checked his aura, and caught nothing but a quick glimpse indicating concentration. At least she'd gotten that much. The continued interruption of a skill she depended upon was not only inconvenient but also scary.

"British potters cornered the market for years," he said. "They exported huge amounts to the U.S., although only a fraction of that amount exists today. That means these plates are a *direct traditional link* to our ancestors. Well, those of us who have British antecedents." He finished off his beer.

She stifled her grin. Score: Jack two, Margaret zip.

"How did you learn about pottery?" Abby asked.

"My mother." He accepted another bottle of beer from Carlos with a nod. "I'm surprised she didn't show off her collection when you were there. She'll love your settings. I think your pattern is somewhat rare."

"Rare? Dang. I wish you hadn't told me that," Abby said.

"Things are meant to be used, Abby," Jack said. "When we let things control us, we forget we're human." He caught Sally's eye. "I've never forgotten the first person to tell me that."

Drowning. She could, and suddenly was, drowning in Jack's gaze and her memories. He'd looked at her the same way before, she'd leapt, and ended up devastated. Not again.

"Well, that's a ridiculous theory," Margaret's Midwestern twang grated. "If we can't determine anything about a person by using the clothes they wear or the car they drive as indicators, how can we know who is worth speaking with?"

Jack snorted and set his beer down. "How, indeed?"

"Well," Margaret sniffed. "It's obvious you aren't very successful in your career. If you were, you'd understand the importance of visible success symbols for establishing contacts with the right people."

A thick silence fell. Sally, Carlos, and Abby exchanged quick glances then all three looked to Jack.

"Yes, I'm sure if I knew the *right people* my life would change."

Abby cleared her throat. "Um, we have dessert and coffee if you all are ready."

Sally helped clear the table, even though Carlos urged her to stay seated. She couldn't remain still one instant more. Not and keep from making a comment to Margaret that she'd regret.

Chapter Twelve

Sally paced the store. What demon had invaded her being? Her full and varied life seemed flat. At the same time, her body itched, like new skin sloughing off the old.

Add her restlessness to regular dealings with Margaret over the past week, and she knew she was mixing a recipe for disaster.

Carlos entered, the stress of having a hypercritical houseguest added to wedding planning showing on his face.

"Sweetie, you need a Mom Hug."

"More than you can guess."

She pulled him to the couch. "What did the Wicked Witch of the Midwest do today?"

"You mean besides being here?" He sighed. "You know I'd do anything for Abby, but having her mother stay with us looks like the worst decision ever made."

"That's a heck of a statement, hon."

He put his head in his hands. "Abby's changing back into the scared person she was when we met. And I don't know how to help her."

"You can remain at her side. That's what couples do. They stick together and talk things out." Not that she could stand as a prime example. She and Jack hadn't done that for their only child.

"We're fine when we're alone. It's like Abby's

riding a seesaw. With me, she's on top, decisive, strong. Then she spends half a day with her mother and she's dragging. Even the dogs are jumpy around her mother. And you know how laidback Henry is."

"Sounds to me as if you need to move Margaret out of the house." She'd watched Abby's mother in action and suspected her real reason for arriving a month early was to stop the wedding. She wouldn't confide her impressions to Abby or her son, but the temptation remained to call Margaret on her actions.

"We tried. She won't go to one of the hotels on the Interstate, and the Blue Peak Inn is booked. Leaf season, remember?"

"Then she can stay with me. She'd still be too close to Abby for comfort, but at least we'd get her out of your house."

"You mean you didn't learn from your trip to Cashiers together?"

She tried to hide a wince and failed. "We hadn't been acquainted long then. Sheesh. How was I to know the curvy mountain roads would make her car sick? Or that a quarter mile paved trail to a waterfall would seem like an uncharted Himalayan trek to her? I'm sure we can arrive at a workable solution."

"Murder is not a workable solution."

"Why did I raise an intelligent kid? I can't get away with anything anymore."

"You're still my favorite mom, even when you're a smart ass."

"That's my favorite son." She cleared her throat. "So I guess you won't help me hide the body? I know some places off trail that would do the trick."

"I wish."

She tapped her forefinger against her lips. "You haven't rented your house yet, right?" Carlos owned a cozy stone-faced bungalow three streets away. "Why don't you move her there?"

"We talked about that at first, but Abby thought her mother might be insulted or feel shuttled-off. Then we invited Abby's dad and new wife to stay there for the wedding."

"Well, there's your answer."

"You mean—"

"Yep. If she thinks she's stealing an advantage, she'll move in a heartbeat."

"You know, I love a devious woman."

"Not devious, astute."

"No matter which word you use, you're a lifesaver."

"Cherry-flavored?"

He laughed. "Any flavor candy you want to be is fine with me." He stood. "I've gotta start lunch prep."

He left and she resumed pacing. The Charlotte concert date loomed. She still hadn't decided how to handle meeting Mitch and the band, or her inconvenient—and growing—attraction to her ex-husband.

Abby had shrugged off her concerns, but her friend didn't know the whole picture. She, Mitch, and the band had been close. After Jack sent papers—when she'd thought he'd initiated the divorce—she'd ended all contact, not that anyone had called more than once. Understanding why didn't ease the old hurt. She closed her eyes. These days, conflict seemed never ending.

\*\*\*\*

Mitch waited with a deceptively lazy pose against

an amplifier stack. "Hey, bro. Got a sec?"

Jack groaned but clapped Mitch on the shoulder. "Anything for you, man. What's up? We still having a sound check, or is it delayed?"

Mitch's thumb rubbed his jaw.

*Shit, now what?*

"Just wondering how it's going with your son, that's all."

His friend's casual air didn't fool him. "Great. I'm standing up at his wedding."

"With Sally?"

He shrugged. "It'll be a small affair."

"The wedding or are you getting back with her?"

"Nothing I'd do with Sally would be small, not that it's your business."

"You know the guys are worried."

"Why, because she's coming along with Carlos and Abby to Charlotte next week? That's a one-night deal."

"Doubt that."

He sighed. "Look, I haven't told you the whole story." He heard a scrape then shuffling footsteps. Checking the area, he saw no one nearby. A second later, the band walked onto the stage for sound check. He looked at his friends and knew he wouldn't be standing there if they hadn't interrupted his downward spiral years before. He owed them.

After telling his buddies the story of how his father had manipulated the divorce and Carlos tracking him down, silence fell.

"Sally and I, well, we screwed up, almost as much as we let ourselves get screwed. Carlos wants us to have a friendly relationship and yeah, I'd like more with Sally. Don't know if that'll happen, but we're talking. We've had dinner together, explored our common ground."

Mitch straightened. "How'd you figure out what happened?"

"Compared notes."

Mitch's fierce gaze sought his like a guided missile. "You're sure that's all?"

"Sure. Look, neither of us wants to make a mistake that would hurt our son. All I'm asking is that you don't shut her out when she comes to Charlotte next week."

The band looked at each other but didn't meet Jack's eyes. His pent-up anger, generated by relating his father's past actions, made his response sound clipped. "Give her a chance. We're trying to be friends for our son's sake."

He didn't want to lose the people who'd stood with him during the worst and best years of his life, but he'd walk away if forced. They meant well, but they couldn't know how desolate his life had become. The rest of them had married and remained with the same women for years.

They studied each other. Tony spoke first. "We want what's best for you, man."

"Thanks." He cleared his throat. "Hey, we've got a sound check, right?"

He picked up his guitar and plucked out a series of chords, drawn into the tones of blue his fingers created. The new song that hadn't gelled before now worked. Once again, he escaped.

After the sound check, he phoned Sally in what had quickly become a pre-show custom. He enjoyed, no craved, the regular contact, their nightly exchange. She entertained him with descriptions of Abby's mother's latest antics. He'd been right. Going on tour had been a blessing in disguise. He'd have used duct tape on Marge long before. In return, he related the high jinx that kept the band from terminal boredom between shows.

Still, he understood that they avoided the tough conversations, both keeping their emotions in check. He hoped they could get past their reluctance to trust. Christ, he sounded like a damn television psychologist.

"Hey, Jack," she answered. "How's wherever you are now treating you? Are the promoters keeping you stocked with premium wines, gourmet foods, and hot women?"

"Tampa. Are you jealous?"

He grinned when she avoided answering by asking another question.

"You getting ready for sound check?"

"Just finished."

"Gonna rock the house tonight?"

"You know it." He changed his tone. "I can't wait to see you all in Charlotte next week." He decided to push the issue. "You are still coming, right? The guys are looking forward to seeing you again. I think some of their wives will be there, too. They've missed you."

She snorted. "Right. Play me another one."

"No, it's true. I spoke with them before the check tonight. They're fine."

"Jack, fine is not the same as 'looking forward to seeing.' Please don't lie. The night is too important to you, and to Carlos, to allow me to ruin. If the band is skeptical, I won't come to Charlotte, and that's that."

Bullshit, if she thought she'd escape that easily. "Don't play the semantics card, professor. Carlos and

Abby want you to be with them. I want you, too. The arrangements have been made. Stop fighting this, already."

"The die is cast," she mumbled.

"What was that?" He'd heard her comment, and knew the reference, but the imp on his shoulder pushed him. "You want to play dice? I guess we could get up a craps game with the roadies."

"Oh, for...never mind. I promised Abby I wouldn't renege, though my spidey senses tell me this is a really bad idea."

"How so? There are likely to be two hundred people backstage. No one will make a big deal out of you three." Well, except for him.

"Will you guarantee that, Jack? Can you? Carlos is confident, but should he be forced to deal with a media onslaught after all these years? He looks too much like you to pass him off as a stranger."

He inhaled sharply. Would all their sacrifices, his agreement to give Sally full custody, be blown in one night? He hadn't thought his ego was in charge over this, but was he using the Charlotte date to show off for his son? Was he that self-involved?

His thoughts sped. He figured asking himself if he acted from ego reassured him that he wasn't, though he owned a need to prove himself to Carlos.

No, he'd make sure nothing went wrong that night. He'd get with Mitch and ask him to limit media access. They'd done it before. The media would keep their special section at the front of the house, and he'd give pre-concert interviews. If he couldn't use his status to make things right for his family now, why'd he walk away then?

"Jack? Are you still on the line?"

"Yeah, sorry, I was thinking. I'll take care of everything." He outlined his plan for limited press access backstage, including assigning them fake names at the security check-in point.

"I guess that's workable," she said.

"Is your intuition really sparking, or are you afraid to face the band?"

She gave a long exhale. "A bit of both, I guess. It's just—"

He waited silently, wishing he could see her face, but she hated Skype. Said it interfered with her intuitive abilities. Abby said Sally couldn't read auras over the small camera. He didn't understand how she could read auras over the phone, either, but didn't ask.

"We both gave up so much. Seeing you again...I've enjoyed our dinners and regular conversations. You get me in a way no other man ever has. It's kind of scary but comfortable at the same time."

"I know." He gulped. Time to pony up. "You've had my back in ways I never knew. Raised my kid to manhood when I'd have done who knows what to him." He reined in his speeding thoughts. "This second chance stuff is iffy. Kind of like déjà vu all over again. Sometimes I think we've got it beat, and other times I know it wouldn't take much to send you running."

He held his breath. Had he said too much, too soon?

"Exactly."

She inhaled, and he sensed she was about to blow his world to bits.

"The thrill isn't gone, Jack, not for me. It's back

and brighter than before."

"Babe, that's what—"

"Wait, let me finish." She sighed. "I see the thrill but that doesn't mean I'm going to hop on the roller coaster. Heights still scare the crap out of me."

"So I won't put you on a pedestal, even though you deserve a freaking throne in the clouds."

"That's not exactly the problem, Jack. I've worked hard, sweetie, and I'm finding it difficult to see how we'll fit together on a daily basis."

Desperation clawed at his heart. "Please, come to Charlotte, You'll see. It'll be good for us. And after this tour ends—"

"You'll still be famous. Jack, we can't meet in public the way normal people do."

"I'd take you any place you wanted, any time, damn the consequences. You like privacy and I like being alone with you."

"Right. Fine."

"Besides, this is my last tour. Everything will calm down once I stop playing."

"Don't you dare stop playing music."

"I won't. It's that…I want time with you, Carlos and Abby. You've heard life is a highway, right? Wanna hitch a ride with me?"

"W-what are you saying?"

"Come to Charlotte with no reservations. Let me show you how good life with me can be. After the tour we can travel to see all those woo-woo places, Stonehenge and the Pyramids. Anywhere in the world you want to go. I'll shave my head and grow a beard. No one will bother us."

His heart pounded as he waited for her answer. A

reply that took a bit too long. "Sally?"

"I've always liked the bald look on men, but don't change for me, Jack. Don't promise me what you may not be able to deliver."

"Carlos's and my interaction has opened a world I never expected or thought I deserved," he said. "Let me do the same for you."

"I'll see you next week, even though I'm afraid of what could happen," Sally said.

"Have you ever had the same feeling about disaster and nothing went wrong?"

"I guess, but I've learned to listen to my intuition. The basic difference between us is that you think life is a highway and I think it's a journey."

He snorted. "Oh, so we're going for bumper sticker slogans to explain our differences?"

"You never believed in the unseen. I can't allow my beliefs to be discounted or ignored." She paused. "That thrill, Jack? I've lived without it for years. Respect is non-negotiable."

"Respect goes both ways. So does trust." A sharp pain hit his chest that he knew was no heart attack. Would they never find peace together? "Can you rely on me?"

"I know you're capable. It's a feeling I have that won't quit. I wish you'd listen."

"I am listening but believe nothing bad will happen."

"Jack, our son looks so much like you at the same age. How will you explain that?"

"You mean this has never come up in the past? No one has ever commented on the resemblance?" He tsked. "Really? So what did you say to those folks?"

"Doppelganger."

"There you go. Good enough for me." He snapped his fingers. "I've got it—we can tell people he's a tribute artist doing research."

"Really?" She copied his tone and phrase. "My—our—son is an original not a copycat."

"Geez, you are wound up. Usually you get my jokes." He rubbed the nape of his neck. "Look, I understand the risk but having you at the concert is a dream come true. I think you're worrying about nothing. But if something does go down, we can face whatever it is together."

Even as he voiced his reply, Jack felt the stirrings of fear cramp his gut. He hoped he hadn't lied.

Chapter Thirteen

Sally sat with her phone in her lap. What in the world had possessed her to tell Jack that she still cared for him? She rubbed her forehead. Nope, she'd said more than that. Holy Baloney.

Besides the media, they needed to deal with Margaret, and explain why they were leaving her behind. Cripes. Nothing about being around Jack was easy.

Of course, that's what made him so attractive.

Their interaction since he'd arrived had drawn them together on more than a social level. They'd met for coffee in Stratton multiple times, had dinner, spoke on the phone daily. They still disagreed on spiritual matters, but Jack had revealed a mind open to many possibilities that made their discussions lively. The way they'd dropped back into being partners, intuiting what the other thought or wanted left her feeling uneasy.

She curled her feet under her on the couch. Stronger, more assured now than at twenty-four, she wasn't afraid to face Jack and demand respect. His raising the trust issue proved to her that he had grown, also. But conflicting, long-held beliefs were difficult to overcome.

Sally had been totally honest with Jack on the phone, and she knew he'd been truthful with her, in return. The problem was that he really didn't believe in her intuition. Nope. Because if he had, he'd have listened to her fears and stopped insisting that they come to Charlotte. Maybe insist was too strong a word. Not really. Jack had always known how to convince her.

His persuasion methods sent her thoughts in a different direction. She shivered with remembered pleasure and then forced concentration on the circumstances they faced.

She dealt with problems through introspection, and suspected he solved issues by throwing cash at a situation. Giving her the world? She had no doubt he'd do so.

Question was, what did she really want?

She hoped her trip to Charlotte would help her decide.

****

A week later, Abby, Carlos, and Sally waited in her living room for the car service Jack had insisted on providing. Earlier today, Bunny and Henry had left for their doggy overnight with friends who owned a small farm and a friendly pack of canines.

"Good thing Margaret had to go back for a condo association meeting," she said. "Otherwise, I had no idea what we'd tell her about leaving her behind."

"I'm sure you'd have thought of something," Abby said. "How you've kept your temper with her has given me hope for world peace."

"Brat."

"I'm serious. You should consider a new career in diplomacy."

"Yes, well, if your mother hadn't gone back to St. Louis, I was about to declare war." She slipped an arm around Abby. "Sweetie, I have no clue how you survived."

"Me, either," Carlos added, lacing his hand with Abby's. "But you're mine, now. Your mother has lightened up since she moved into my house, but I'm watching. One more thoughtless jibe from her and I'll set her straight. I've held back because you insisted, but I won't allow her abuse."

"She's not deliberately abusive, she's—"

"Angry and bitter and needs a life outside you." Sally squeezed her shoulders. "She wants love but she won't allow any to touch her. That's easy to see. I'll keep sending her positive vibes and hope for the best. But I'm with Carlos. One more crack and she'll hear from me."

A quick rap sounded at the door.

Sally jumped. "The driver. Come on, you two."

She felt light-headed, a problem that may have been avoided had she been able to eat. She'd hoped for a quick meditation before leaving, but Carlos and Abby had walked over early. Perhaps the two plus hour drive would give her time to relax her jumpy nerves.

But the journey seemed to take less time than she'd expected or hoped. They pulled up behind the auditorium, and the driver escorted them to the door. She panicked. What name was she supposed to use?

Carlos glanced at her, stepped up and gave their names to the bulked-up security guard blocking the entrance.

The guard checked his board. He looked them over, eyed the driver who accompanied them, and opened the door. "Give your name at the table and you'll get passes. Have a nice night."

She fumbled with her purse, looking for the tip she'd meant to give the driver. When she turned with the cash, he held up his hand. "All handled, but thanks for thinking of me."

"Wait." Her pulse had sped up the closer they'd gotten to the concert site. "Will you be driving us back tomorrow? What time should we be ready?"

"I'm at your disposal." He tipped his hat, and walked to the car, whistling.

Did that mean she could jump in the car and return to Blue Peak right now? Because that's what she wanted. Her desire to see Jack play again warred with the unknown reception the rest of the Rough Cuts would give her.

She inhaled a deep breath. Too late now. She turned and walked into the building.

Two people stood before a table staffed by a man with another clipboard. When she heard the young woman identify herself, her wish to escape intensified. Cristal Shaw. Jack and that groupie's child. What had been the groupie's name?

"Glynnis McKinney." The woman's voice was low, sexually-charged. The guard blinked then handed them each a pass.

*Crap. What game did Jack play?*

Sally signed the roster, unsure whether she used the pseudonym or her real name. Her writing was little more than a scrawl, so she doubted it would matter. The guard was too busy watching Glynnis walk away to check closely.

Not that she blamed him. The woman's strawberry blonde hair curled in long waves down her back, almost reaching her waist. She wore tight leather pants, a cropped multi-colored silk top, and what looked like designer heels. Her over-sized handbag bumped against her hip, emphasizing her runway model movements. Birthing a child twenty-two years ago hadn't slowed her down. Not as it had Sally.

She glanced down at the short black dress, spangled jacket and glittery scarf she'd chosen. Her feet were cramped in the matching stilettos she'd worn. She'd wished now that she'd kept to her normal flowing garb. At least she'd be comfortable in an already difficult situation.

Abby touched her shoulder. "Are you okay? You should have eaten more than a few crackers today." She handed her a laminated card attached to a lanyard sporting the Rough Cuts' logo. The card, printed in color with a complicated background read "BAND."

Sally shook her head. "What? Yes, I'm fine. Does Carlos know how to find Jack?" She had a few choice words for him. Waiting to deliver them was not an option.

"I'm not sure, but the Green Room is ahead to the left. The guard mentioned something about a sound check starting in a minute. These passes give us full access." She tilted her head. "Are you sure you're okay?"

"Yep." Her smile stretched tight lips.

"You look gorgeous, classy. Wearing your hair up with a few curls around your face really emphasizes your eyes. Jack will have a freaking heart attack."

"I hope not, for Carlos's sake. Let's move on." She ignored Abby's smirk, waved Carlos over, and headed for the Green Room.

They were directed to the stage wings. Jack's gaze

caught hers and tangled. He smiled and played the opening chords to the hit from their first album. It was a song he'd written while they were married, one he'd said she inspired. The band hadn't played "Eyes of Love" in public since that first tour.

Her knees weakened. She felt Carlos put his arm around her shoulder while Abby took her hand. The melody and lyrics wrapped themselves around her. No wonder no other man had ever made a dent in her heart. She'd never stopped loving Jack. Even with her anger piqued, she was willing to listen. And he had a lot of explaining to do tonight.

The stage lights kicked in, making it impossible to read auras, not that her skill had returned with any consistency. She had to rely on Tony's friendly nod to know that she was welcomed by at least one band member. Mitch hadn't shown, but he had to be close.

They completed the song. She could tell the band was charged Jack had pulled out the old number.

"What say we add that to tonight's play list," Tony called. "I always liked that song."

She felt her muscles loosen when the rest of the band agreed and they moved on to another tune. Perhaps tonight wasn't a total mistake. Or maybe she shouldn't let down her guard.

Jack ambled to the wings, drew her close and planted a long, hot kiss on her lips.

Abby held her hand out to Carlos. "I was right. Pay up."

Her son sent her an accusing glare. "You two are getting it on?"

Her face heated. "No. We're not involved in anything but a friendship."

Carlos narrowed his eyes at her.

Simultaneously, Jack said, "You don't mind if I date your mother, do you?"

Abby wiggled her fingers in front of Carlos's face. "It's only a matter of time. Jack knows what he wants. You may as well pay up."

A tech rushed past with extra cords dangling from his hands.

"This is not the best place for a private conversation," Sally said.

"Yeah, right." Jack took her arm. "Let's go to my dressing room. I thought you'd like a private meeting with the guys."

Her shoulders were up around her ears when he opened the door. Only the band waited. She felt like Yoko must have facing the Beatles.

Jack's hand was at the small of her back, nudging her inside. She took a deep breath and smiled. Tony approached and drew her into a bear hug. Before long, everyone was pulling out pictures and sharing information about their wives, children, and grandchildren.

A knock sounded and Mitch stuck his head in the room. You guys ready? I've got the press waiting down the hall. Jack gave her a smoldering look followed with a heated kiss, then left. Her legs were shaky but she hadn't messed up. Thank Goddess. She sat, removed her shoes and wiggled her toes.

"The caterer finished setting up in the Green Room," Carlos said. "Abby and I are going to get something to eat. Do you want us to bring you something back?"

Now that the first meeting was over, she felt ready

to eat. "Sure. Anything. Thanks."

Mitch entered as they left. They eyed each other over the gulf of bad memories.

"So? Are you going to stick with Jack this time?"

She ignored his barely veiled aggressive tone. "We're working things out at Carlos's request. We're friends, and that's all the further we've gotten." She shifted to look Mitch full in the face. "Besides, I'd like to get things straight with Jack first if you don't mind."

"The moves he put on you just now sure looked like you've already gotten *straight* with him."

"Not your business, Mitch." She sighed. "I'd hoped we could be friends, too. I appreciated the way you watched out for the band."

"Yeah, like you cared after you dumped Jack."

"I didn't—"

He waved his hand. "Never mind. Some memories die hard." He worried a thumbnail. "Jack told me what happened with his father." He rubbed his hand over his wiry gray hair. "Look, I don't have much time. I want to know if you're serious about being with Jack, or if I need to keep a closer eye on him again."

Her heart stopped beating. "Do what?"

Mitch studied her face before answering. "You really don't know what happened on that first tour, do you?"

"I blocked out most of that time, but I heard he partied non-stop. Now Jack and I talk mostly about Carlos and what he missed being gone." She narrowed her eyes. "What's this about?"

"I'll tell you if you think you're ready."

She nodded, the lump in her throat preventing her from answering.

"Jack almost died, that's what happened."

She slumped in her chair. Her knuckles turned white.

Mitch nodded. "I wondered if you knew. After he got the divorce papers, he went off the deep end. He hurt bad."

Her panic turned to anger. "Why didn't you call me? I would have come."

"We did and you didn't answer. I thought—we all did—that you walked out and took Carlos without saying a word, remember?" He scratched his head. "We knew that Jack couldn't reach you. If you wouldn't let him know where his son was, why would you tell us?" He rubbed his chin. "We figured you were a stone cold bitch."

Sally recoiled from his words. Her damn stubbornness and pride had kept her from following Jack's career. Hard enough to listen through the door when Carlos became a Rough Cuts fan. She'd refused to read about Jack for years, even canceled their subscription to *Rolling Stone* after seeing the groupie photo. Once she'd entered academia, avoiding the rock and roll world had been easy. She'd had no idea he'd been in trouble, but would she really have traveled to help him at the beginning? The sad answer came fast. No. She wouldn't have exposed their son to the scene.

"How did you turn him around?"

Mitch leaned forward, his forearms on his knees. "The band did that. After the tour, they told him he'd get thrown out on his ass unless he settled down. Got him into rehab. Music is the only other thing Jack has ever loved."

"Wait a minute. Rehab? Couldn't have worked.

Jack still drinks. I've seen him."

"No more than a couple of beers, some wine. His substance abuse wasn't a sign of an addictive personality but a reaction. He dealt with his loss and the abuse stopped."

She dropped her gaze to study her hands. Jack hadn't had the opportunity to fully deal with his loss until recently. Given the appearance of Cristal and Glynnis tonight, she suspected he still hadn't forgiven her. What a karmic mess.

"So now you see why I'm a little antsy about his inviting you here."

She nodded, too shaken with Jack's history to answer.

Mitch reached to lightly tap her white knuckles. "We loved you, Sally. The whole Rough Cuts group. You didn't just walk out on Jack, you left all of us. I'm not so sure his dating you is such a hot idea, but we're all glad Jack is getting to know his son."

Tension glued her hands to the armrests. She forced herself to speak through tight lips. "Don't worry. We're creating a friendship, not dating. Even if he and I don't…he'll always have Carlos and Abby."

"Good." Mitch rose and started for the door.

"Mitch?"

He swiveled.

"Thanks for sticking with Jack and saving his life."

A red flush stole up his neck. "I told you, the band did that."

"Yeah, but you planted the seeds."

He walked out, leaving the door open behind him. She hoped that move wasn't an invitation for her to leave.

Chapter Fourteen

"Jack, we've heard this is your last tour. Care to comment?"

The low-hum of chatter died. He sipped his water, buying time.

"You know this wasn't supposed to be a Rough Cuts tour. We're filling in for Steddi Eddi."

Another reported followed-up with a shout. "So are you going out on a longer tour next year to promote your new album?"

Jack glanced to the side. Tony barely shook his head. "We haven't decided."

More questions that he didn't want to answer about touring came from the media. The band took turns deflecting the inquiries, but the reporters stayed on track, like the predators they too often resembled.

He waited for Mitch to intervene, but their manager was nowhere in sight. Who blabbed and where the hell was Mitch?

Jack whistled to get everyone's attention. "Look, we haven't made up our minds about a tour, so let's move on. Asking us the same question ten different ways won't change our answers."

He glanced at the door as Mitch walked in.

The same man who'd asked the first tour question called to Tony, who nodded a go ahead. "We heard you're resurrecting old songs for tonight's show. Any special reason why?"

Jack felt a cold shiver travel his spine. The guy's questions were a touch too close to his secret.

Tony shrugged. "We'll play both old and new, the way we always do."

Mitch approached with his hands in the air. "We've gotta wrap this up." He pointed to two reporters who asked general questions about their current tour. Five minutes later, he ushered them from the dais to the Green Room.

He wanted to ask Sally if her spidey sense had gone on alert, or if his itchy feeling was an unusual nervousness. He'd like to hold her close and kick back before the show. That wasn't possible with the number of people milling around. Not and keep Carlos's and her identities safe from nosey people.

Glynnis wrapped her arms around his waist. "Hey, Jack. Long time no fuck."

He unhooked her arms and stepped away. "I'd say it was nice to see you again, but I'd be lying. How'd you get in here? I sure as hell didn't put you on the guest list."

She pouted. "Jack, don't be mean." Her hand rubbed his chest and moved south. "I came tonight to see you."

He snorted and grabbed her roving hand. "Right. Like I care."

Her eyes widened. "It's true. We were good together. You know I can give head like no one else. You said so."

"Long time ago, Glynnis. Not making the return trip."

"No? You sure?" She pulled his head down and

planted her lips on his, pushing her tongue into his mouth. Her body plastered against his, her hips moving against him in a sultry, yet demanding thrust.

Taken aback at her quick move, Jack froze. Camera flashes popped around them. Pushing away from the embrace, he willed himself not to visually react. Glancing to where he'd last seen Sally, he noted that her back was to him.

He brushed Glynnis's hand from his chest. "I said no. Go find someone else, preferably not our head technician this time." He looked at the floor. *Damn.* He shouldn't have said that, but she'd pushed her luck.

Her face whitened. Her lips narrowed. "Fine. You don't have to be nasty." She straightened and assumed a sexy pose. Her lips curved into a smile, but her eyes glinted. She ran her fingertips over his lips. "Bye, sugar."

Tony tapped him on the shoulder. "Jack, I want you to meet someone."

Shaken, he chatted with the man, a music teacher from a local school. After the instructor moved off, he rubbed his forehead, hoping Sally hadn't seen that bullshit with Glynnis go down.

Momentarily free of people demanding his attention, he snagged a bottle of water, caught Sally's eye over the crowd and winked. Her lack of response, rather, her stoic appearance left him reeling. The night he'd waited weeks to experience wasn't playing out the way he wanted. Then she flashed him a quick smile filled with heat and promise. He relaxed and returned to the meet and greet so familiar to his pre-concert routine.

Jack stood a few paces behind his family, watching the warm-up band troop in after finishing their set. The band was better than Mitch had said. He felt good about making this his last tour and insisting on keeping the information quiet. If he hadn't, these guys would have been ignored in the hoopla.

As the Cuts waited to take the stage, he stood behind Sally, his palm caressing her butt. She jumped and looked over her shoulder. Seeing him there, she smiled.

"Rock the house, big boy."

"All for you, Sally." He whispered in her ear, his hand on her back. "I have a surprise for you. Listen for it."

He moved beside Carlos, clapping his hand his son's shoulder while waiting for his cue. As the announcer yelled out, "Charlotte welcomes the Rough Cuts." Carlos leaned close. "Kick butt, Dad."

He'd picked a hell of a place to call him Dad for the first time.

Heart pounding, he ran onstage pumping his fist. The crowd roared. He picked up his guitar and sent the distinctive "Eyes of Love's" opening chords back at them. The audience jumped to their feet and stayed there. Jack's searing guitar licks pushed the crowd higher. Tony punched the beat and held them together as the band cooked stronger than they had on their last two tours. They knew they were creating a singular night, and the fans did their part.

Later in the set, he settled on a stool to play the new acoustic solo. A quick glance to the wings, revealed Carlos at Sally's side with his arms around both her and Abby's shoulders. Cristal and Glynnis stood beside them. Carlos's resemblance to his younger self, the dim lights creating a youthful glow around

Sally, and her shining expression made his heart stutter. They'd wasted so damn much time.

"This is a new song." He waited for the applause to die down. "I'm dedicating this to the special people in my life." He caught Sally's eye. "No one will ever replace you."

Jack finished the song, and then traded out his Olson SJ for the Strat. Tony's sticks counted the tempo and kicked off the tune that would end the set. He glanced to the wings to gauge Sally's reaction.

She was gone.

\*\*\*\*

When Jack announced the new song, Glynnis had bumped Sally's arm with her elbow. She leaned over and spoke in her ear. "Nice of Jack to dedicate this to me and our kid, isn't it?" She smirked then blew a kiss toward the stage.

When Sally glanced his way, Jack was bent over the guitar, seemingly lost in the song. Had she misinterpreted his look and words as meant for herself, Carlos and Abby? Anger stirred in her gut. Had Jack changed, or did he think he could have a family and groupie sex on the road, too? She'd seen Glynnis latch on to Jack like a boa constrictor around its prey. It hadn't looked as if he'd invited the embrace, but she hadn't watched long. The image of Glynnis trying to swallow Jack whole had made her throat dry. She'd had to blink back tears and maintain her smile in the midst of strangers. Not her favorite occupation.

She worked to calm her nerves and distrust as Glynnis moved two steps away and linked arms with Cristal. Jack and that woman had a daughter together, if the stories were true. Jack had never denied the rumors.

He hadn't confirmed them either which had always given her pause.

Sally ducked her son's arm, moving to leave. He stopped her with a hand on her arm.

"Dad wrote this for us. You can't walk away."

She glanced at Glynnis. "The lights are messing with my vision. I'll listen from further back in the wings."

He frowned but turned back to listen, pulling Abby closer.

An itching sensation in her throat told her she needed to move before tears revealed how much Glynnis's words had hurt.

She couldn't believe Jack had singled them out. The fans and media couldn't see Carlos, but others had. The back of her neck tingled. That move had not been smart. Neither had Carlos calling Jack "Dad." Flirting with danger, the two of them, especially with strangers within listening distance. Besides that, the look Jack had thrown their way had jarred her core. At least until Glynnis had claimed it for herself.

Listening to the monitors, looking out at the first rows of the audience, blinded to the rest but knowing by the noise level the place was packed and rocking, Sally understood Jack in a way she hadn't before. This was his world, the onslaught of cheers and applause, the palpable wave of love, belonged to, no, sustained him. How could one person's love replace a crowd's? Jack's world, his reality overwhelmed her.

She waited until the song ended, then took off for Jack's dressing room, knowing the first set would end with the next song.

Avoiding the chair she'd sat in during her

conversation with Mitch, she plopped onto the couch, toeing off her shoes and closing her eyes. She quickly calmed her breathing, hoping her intuition would pop. The only message she received was one she'd rather not have heard. "Prepare for difficulty."

"Shit." She should have stayed and accepted Jack's dedication, listened to his song, instead of running like a Greyhound at the starting bell. An apology wouldn't work. She'd have to grovel, at least.

"What's the matter? Couldn't stand that Jack dedicated a song to me?"

She raised her gaze. Glynnis stood at the door.

"Sudden headache," Sally lied. "I'm not used to loud music anymore."

"Yeah, I understand older people have that problem." She leaned against the molding and crossed her arms. "So, who are you, exactly?"

"An older person who received a free pass. Like you." The woman frowned. "Getting a free concert pass, I mean."

"Maybe you don't know that Jack and I hook up when he's in town."

Sally kept her face as expressionless as possible. "Good for you."

Her eyes narrowed into slits. "I don't think we've met. I'm Glynnis." Her arms remained crossed over her chest.

Sally nodded. She hadn't been a player in academia for nothing. Her ability to snub had been equaled to "a Dowager Duchess in a snit" by a British professor buddy. "How nice for you." She closed her eyes. "I hope you don't mind if I relax. My head is killing me."

"Relax somewhere else. This is Jack's dressing

room. He likes his privacy."

Sally opened one eye. "I think he'll be okay with me here."

Glynnis jutted her hips forward. "He may want a quickie between sets. Wanna watch?"

Sally yawned. "I can't believe you'd settle for a quickie. If I had Jack in my bed, I'd want him all night long. And more than once." She shut her eyes. "A lot to be said for waiting."

She knew Glynnis remained in the doorway but wouldn't play her game. The music ended, and loud cheers rang the auditorium, including backstage. She didn't want to be in a standoff when Jack returned. Not when she meant to apologize the minute she saw him.

Sally sighed and straightened. "I'm an *old* friend of Jack's. I knew him before you were born." For some inexplicable reason, she felt sorry for Glynnis. "Jack should be here any second. I need to speak with him, then he's all yours."

Jack appeared in the entrance. "No, I'm not all hers." He motioned to a guard. "Keep everyone away from my door."

Sally's stomach jumped. Time to clear the air. She stood, her hands shaking.

He pushed past Glynnis. "Why'd you run after I dedicated a song to you? What game are you playing?" He slammed the door, but not before both the guard and Glynnis heard his words.

She knew he was past angry by the low, intense tone of his voice. "I got scared, Jack. I didn't want anyone discovering Carlos's identity."

His eyes narrowed. "There's more. I saw Glynnis talking to you. What did she say?" He took two steps then stopped, as if he'd finally absorbed her words. "Damn it. Do we have to have the trust argument again?"

"No. I heard Carlos call you dad, and Glynnis was standing almost on top of us. Security was close, too. I listened to your song, all of it, standing further back in the wings." She pushed her curls from her face. "I loved it."

He moved closer. "That new song was my surprise for you."

"I thought 'Eyes of Love' was what you meant. Thank you. For both."

He twined a lock of her hair around his finger. "That's all I get for writing you a new song about a lost love?"

"Glynnis told me you wrote it for her."

"That bitch. What was she saying when I got here?"

"That you wanted a quickie, and I should take my old bones home."

He grabbed a towel and rubbed the back of his neck and face. "Fuck."

"Jack, is this your way of preventing problems?"

"Shit. Tony told me Cristal would show, but he thought it'd be tomorrow night, and he sure didn't know Glynnis would come along as a plus one."

"So what's she doing here?"

"Don't worry about her. She'll get bored and leave."

She couldn't see his aura—no surprise—but didn't need proof to know he lied. "She wants to hook up with you again." She held her breath.

He shrugged. "Not gonna happen."

Sally released her breath. She raised her eyebrows. "I don't own you, Jack."

"Yes, you do." He shook his head. "You've got my heart all wrapped up, and you don't believe me."

She pushed aside her fear and asked the question uppermost in her mind. "What's the truth about Glynnis and Cristal, Jack? I need to know."

He pulled her down to the couch. "I banged Glynnis, yeah, but Cristal's not mine."

Her eyes searched his, looking for confirmation to his words. "How can you be sure?"

"Trust me. It's impossible." He rubbed his jaw.

She nodded. His tone was certain, yet she intuited he hid a key part of the story. "Okay. Then what emotional hold does she have over you?"

"There is no hold, but there is dirty history." A grimace flashed across his face.

"Trust goes both ways." Her intuition told her whatever he held back could change their relationship. Forever. She gentled her tone. "If you want to tell me, I'll listen with an open mind. Honest."

His shoulders slumped. "Nasty story. Sure you want to hear it?"

She braced herself. "Yes, because I think you've been holding in whatever happened for way too long."

"Yeah. Guess I have." He laced his fingers with hers. "Our lead tech back then, Billy Hatter, was a technical guru. We called him the Mad Hatter because he was a fucking genius with the boards. Too bad his genius didn't extend to people. He was naïve. When Glynnis came on to him after screwing everyone else, he thought he'd found true love."

Her forehead crinkled in a frown. "So what'd that

have to do with you? I know your sense of loyalty. You wouldn't touch another man's woman. Not knowingly."

The corners of his mouth rose. "Thanks." His lips thinned. "There's more. Should I keep going?"

She nodded.

"Even though Billy knew me for years, he trusted Glynnis when she told him she was pregnant and the kid was mine."

She tightened her hand around his.

"Billy stayed on working the tour, but things weren't right between us. I didn't know the problem until later." He rubbed the back of his neck. "Anyway, after the last show, he took off soon as he could, but not before taking a bottle of booze or two with him and leaving a note for me." He clenched his eyes, his forehead a mass of wrinkles. "They found him the next morning. He'd lost control on a curve, hit a tree less than a mile from his home."

"How is that your fault? Did you force him to drink a bottle of booze? Or drive too fast?"

He met her gaze. "You don't get it. I should have pushed him to tell me what was wrong. Should have insisted he talk with me. Instead, I figured he had a bug up his butt, and he could go hang. He died because I didn't care enough. I was too busy partying."

"Guilt is baloney. What other adults choose to do is not your responsibility." She grabbed Jack's shoulders and shook gently. "I want you to understand this with your heart along with your head. The person at fault in all this is Glynnis. She lied and betrayed Billy's trust. She used you. Her karma is shit. Trust me on this."

A glint of humor lit his eyes. "You're my go-to person for metaphysical crap."

"Don't try changing the subject. What's the rest of the story?"

If she'd had any doubts about why he'd left Carlos behind, they were erased, even though she'd once have staked her life that Jack was capable of carelessly walking away from his child to further his career. That had been ignorance and hate talking, and she was far from feeling hate right now. In fact, his proximity and the warm breath on her neck made her head spin.

"Glynnis brought suit naming me as father and the rest is old news."

Sally hoped she didn't sputter like a cartoon character, but she suspected the worst. She inhaled hoping to calm her pounding heart. "Why wasn't the truth revealed? The story about Cristal's birth made you look like a...a...I don't know, self-absorbed asshole for years."

"You think you're the only person who likes their privacy?" He squeezed her hand. "Sorry, babe. Truth is, Billy's mother wasn't well. She died not long after he did. There was no one else to look after Cristal."

"So you paid up because you blamed yourself for Billy's death."

He finished off his water. "People expect and want celebrities to have problems. I could handle the press better than a kid."

"I see," she said.

"My lawyers wrote an iron-clad settlement agreement. If Glynnis poisoned Cristal's knowledge about Billy or ever talked to the press, she'd lose a bundle of cash. Then Tony stepped in. He and Liz adopted Billy's child, giving her a loving home. Cristal knows the truth. We've never lied to her."

He ran his finger down her cheek. "That's the story. Cristal is an awesome kid. I want you, Carlos and Abby to meet her."

Her emotions, already sparked by Jack's story, ignited under his lingering touch. "I'd love to know her."

"She's grown up with the band's kids. They ran in a pack when younger, but her best friend is Dougie's youngest kid, who lives here in Charlotte."

Not all of the kids. Carlos never had that familiarity. Trust. Her lack of trust had deprived their son of a special life, filled with more than she could ever give him, and other kids to share his upscale life. Once again, she wished she could change her past choices.

She squelched her guilt. "So what's with Glynnis showing the same night as me?"

Jack shrugged. "She shows up once or twice a tour. We put up with her because everyone loves Cristal. Not her fault she's got a messed up birth mother."

"I don't believe in coincidences."

"The universe has plans, yeah, I remember. Destiny." Jack's fingertips grazed her jaw. "I know what I want fate to bring me tonight, and I hope you'll join me."

She caught her breath. The temptation in his eyes was clear. She knew they'd been approaching this crossroads since their first meeting in Carlos's office. A chill ran down her spine.

"The suite has three bedrooms. I'm hoping we'll only need two of them." He played with the curls at her temple. "One for Abby and Carlos, and one for us."

She answered before her nerves kicked in further.

"Yes. I'll share your room."

His eyes darkened, He rubbed her lips with his thumb. "You will?"

She nodded. "And your bed."

He replaced his thumb with his lips, his long fingers framing her face. His tongue thrust into her mouth, and hers met his in a wet tangle. She entered the heat and lost herself in the maelstrom Jack's lips on hers created.

They had moved halfway to madness when pounding on the door interrupted their increasingly heated kisses.

Jack lifted his lips from hers and groaned. His head turned toward the door. "Go away," he shouted. "I'm busy."

"You bet your ass you are," Mitch said. "On stage. One minute."

"Shit." Jack rested his hands on her shoulders, his forehead against hers. "You're coming back to hear the rest of the show, aren't you?"

"You bet your fine butt I am."

Mitch pounded on the door. "Jack. Get out here."

"Coming." He unfolded his length and stood, pulling her up beside him. His mouth to her ear he said, "Not coming yet, but I hope we will tonight."

"You're impossible."

He ran his thumbs across her lips. "I love that stern professor look you get."

More pounding. "Jack. Now."

He slid his fingers into her hair and moved his lips over hers, sucking her tongue into his mouth. Then he brushed his palms over her breasts. Her nipples hardened. The kiss that followed robbed her breath.

Jack pulled away, threw open the door and walked past Mitch. "Quit your bitching. You and I both know you roust me five minutes before I'm due back."

Mitch took in her tousled appearance. He shook his head and followed Jack.

She smoothed her hair and ran a trembling hand down her wrinkled dress. Wow. She wasn't sure whether to kick her own butt or celebrate. The die was cast, all right. In spades.

Glynnis sauntered past and sneered while casting a practiced eye over Sally's rumpled appearance. Sally noted however, that the woman moved to the opposite wings for the rest of the show. Good thing.

A second set and multiple encores later, the band relaxed in the Green Room. Media were excluded, so the group, although large, had the camaraderie peculiar to a band and their crew.

The caterer had replenished the food and drink. Sally still had no stomach for either, though everything on offer was top notch. She reflected that while Jack lived the high life, she was more comfortable with her quiet existence. She couldn't give Carlos what Jack could provide, but that was the point. Quality food and drink, limousines, fawning people, and notoriety wasn't what she wanted for herself, but to deny Carlos the opportunity to decide how much of that he wished to experience wasn't her responsibility, and hadn't been for a long time.

Jack's heat warmed her side as they sat together on a couch. Her heart held doubts. Was she willing to give up her privacy yet exist in Jack's shade? She wasn't sure, but Jack cast a huge shadow. No one would notice her there. She gave herself a mental palm slap. Right.

Like that would happen given the circumstances.

Cristal perched on the sofa's arm next to Jack.

"Hi, Jack, who's your friend?"

"Cristal, meet Sally."

They leaned across Jack and shook hands. Sally immediately liked the young woman's enthusiasm. She knew if she could see auras again, that hers would contain mostly joy.

Cristal pointed to Carlos. "Who's the dude? He looks like a young Jack but hotter."

Sally replied "doppelganger," while Jack simultaneously said "tribute artist." She nudged his ribs. He gave her an unrepentant smirk. "That's my son," Sally said. "I'd like you to meet him if you have a minute."

"He single?"

"Nope, engaged. That's his fiancée, Abby, next to him."

Cristal grinned. "Too bad. I like older dudes."

Jack hugged her waist. "You mean me, right? Your favorite uncle?"

"Yeah, right," she smirked. "So what's the story with you two? I wondered because you're sitting a little too close to each other for friend friends." She pointed to Sally. "I figure I know who you really are, not that anyone is talking."

"No one but you, loud mouth." Jack ruffled her hair.

"Hey, I'm not a kid." She rolled her eyes and smoothed her hair. She caught Sally's eye. "Men."

They shared a grin. "We can count on you to keep our secret, right?" Sally asked.

"Yep, I like your look. Classy. Not like some

people I know." Her glance moved to her birth mother, who stood across the room flirting with a roadie. She put her arm around Jack's shoulders and hugged. Her head against his, she said, "I couldn't say no to bringing Glynnis in tonight."

"You know I'm not angry about your plus one."

The young woman addressed Sally. "I saw her talking with you. I hope she didn't give you a hard time."

"Never apologize for someone else's actions, or for being compassionate. And she didn't say anything I couldn't handle," Sally said.

"I believe that. I'm glad you're taking this old man on. You're strong enough to bust his ego chops, and he needs a family." She stood. "Guess I'll go introduce myself to my almost brother." She walked off, calling over shoulder. "Later, old fart."

Sally blinked. "Wow. She's vibrant."

"Yep, like her dad. Both of them." He fingered her curls. "Ready to leave for the hotel?" He faked a large yawn. "I'm ready for bed."

"If you're going to crash, I'll use that third bedroom."

He lowered his voice. "I'm not sleeping until we've had Smurf sex."

"What?"

"I want to screw you until we're blue in the face." He lowered his voice. "I won't quit until you've had multiple orgasms."

She struck a thoughtful pose. "Multiple, as in two?"

He snorted. "Multiple as in personal best."

Her face heated. She knew he meant a night when

they'd lost count. She'd avoided a bladder infection but walked stiffly for two days. "How are you planning to carry that off? Have you taken a little pill?"

His forehead wrinkled. The corners of his lips turned down. "I don't need pharmaceuticals to show you how I feel. We've got too many empty nights behind us for me to slack off now."

She put her hand on his arm. "Then why don't we set a new personal best tonight and work on improving that number through time?"

He drew in a sharp breath. "An excellent idea, Professor Ford. I think I'll like being your student."

"Maybe not. I'm a tough grader."

"Then I'll work harder."

"Are you two flirting?" Carlos stood before them, his arm around Abby.

"No," Sally said.

"Yes," replied Jack.

Carlos looked at them each in turn. "I'd guess we're about to leave for the hotel."

Jack and she spoke together. "You always were my smartest son."

Chapter Fifteen

Mitch hustled up, his forehead dripping sweat. He pulled Jack to the side. "Jack, man I'm sorry."

Jack's good mood faded. Whatever Mitch had to say had better not screw with his plans for a hotel bed with Sally. Sooner than later. "What's wrong?"

"The press, they're waiting at the door."

His forehead wrinkled. "Why? We gave them interviews. They should be filing stories on the concert about now." His stomach dropped. No, couldn't be.

"Somehow they found out about Carlos. And Sally. Security is keeping them from inside the building, but not the premises."

Damn. He glanced at his ex-wife. Her face held a worried expression, as if she knew a problem had arisen. "Shit. I should have listened to Sally."

"Hell, you shoulda listened to me, first," Mitch said. "Always leave the past behind."

"Mitch, if I did that, I wouldn't have any songs, much less a career."

"Yeah, there is that." Mitch rubbed both hands over his wiry hair.

"So, how are we handling this?"

"My office will issue a statement in the morning. You can duck questions until then. Unless you want to hide out until we leave town without making a statement? Or I could schedule another press conference. Up to you, man."

"Those are my only options?"

"Nah, you could talk to the media camped around the gates. They're probably at the hotel, too."

"The options suck."

"Yeah, I know. First, get your family out of here. Security will take you out the front. No one will expect you to leave that way. Once you get to the suite, talk together. Decide how you want to handle the press. I'll alert my office. They'll act at your call."

"Thanks, Mitch." He turned to go. "And Mitch?"

"Yeah."

"I want to know what dickweed leaked this. I don't care who it is—I don't ever want to see them around me, or my family, again. Got it?"

"Already on it. I'm checking several leads."

"Knew I could count on you."

\*\*\*\*

Sally suspected trouble brewed the instant she saw Jack and Mitch huddle. Their worried looks only underscored the intuitive messages that had screamed without stop for days.

At a signal from Mitch, several security guards appeared in the doorway. They shepherded the small group to the front door. The guards checked the exterior then held open the building doors as a limo, followed by a large SUV, pulled around the corner at a quick pace. Hurrying to the curb, the group piled into the vehicles and sped off.

"Geez, I feel like we're in a spy flick. What the hell is going on?" Carlos asked.

Jack flicked a glance at the driver. "We'll talk in the suite."

Their ride to the hotel took short minutes. Once there, the security guards checked the area, then led them in through a back door held open by a man whose tag proclaimed him the night manager. From there it was a tense ride up the service elevator to their floor. Jack held a short, quiet conversation with the guards. He locked the door and turned to face them, his face gray and his posture slumped.

"Someone figured out that Carlos is your son, didn't they." Sally wasn't asking. She'd arrived at the obvious deduction during the ride.

"Christ, nothing I do where you're concerned is right, Carlos." Jack sank onto the couch. "Damned no matter which way I move."

Carlos sat next to his father, while Abby perched on the sofa arm. Sally admired the picture they made while choosing a seat across from them. Media attention was the last thing she'd wanted. Had they lived their lonely solo lives in vain?

She moved to the coffee table in front of Jack and took his hands in hers. "Sweetie, how bad is it? Did Mitch say?"

Jack shook his head. "Bad. A media horde at the arena doors and another waiting outside the hotel." His Adam's apple moved as he swallowed. "Must be a slow news day."

She tightened her grip on his hands. "Sure, this has nothing to do with you being a big freaking star who's already been accused of fathering a daughter. Or the famous women you've been involved with in the past." She snorted. "An until now unknown family of a rock megastar? Who the hell would care about that?"

Jack grinned. "You always know how to put things

into perspective." His calloused thumbs caressed the backs of her hands. She felt herself slip into the familiar Jack vortex, where the world receded.

"So are we captive here?" Her voice raised on the last word.

"No, not at all, but if you want to stay for the show tomorrow night, I'd love for you to be there."

She pulled her hands from his. "Right. So the media can get another shot at Carlos."

"You could wear disguises. Carlos could dye his hair green. I think the hotel can provide the Jello, or is it Kool-Aid?"

She didn't ask how he knew about temporary hair coloring. "Sure, and we could wear latex masks, or dress like Kiss imitators. That'll work."

"Mom, I think Dad feels bad enough. Let's figure out where we go from here," Carlos said.

She rubbed her chest. Hearing Jack referred to as "Dad" by their son added another layer of emotion to the evening. Emotion she couldn't and didn't want to identify.

Jack threw her a smile but spoke to Carlos. "Your mom and I always used humor and sarcasm to work out problems. I still do, in fact, remember our first conversation? I can handle her comments." He fake punched Carlos in the shoulder. "But, thanks for sticking up for me."

He quickly outlined Mitch's options for dealing with the press. Sally figured their son had the most at risk, so rather than joining in, she watched the other three strategize.

"Why so quiet, babe? You've got a stake in this, too."

Jack's question gave her pause. "What do you mean? What you all think best for Carlos works for me."

He leaned forward, crowding her space. "Don't turn your back on this situation. You'll be as much an object of curiosity as our son."

\*\*\*\*

Sally's expression tightened as Jack's words hit home. His hope for a future with her dropped into a dark place at the pit of his stomach. He could kick himself for stupidity, but the truth couldn't be hidden. She'd have seen the obvious for herself. He should have kept his mouth shut.

Carlos and Abby jumped into the silence, debating which of their choices would be least invasive. After a surprisingly short discussion, the group found consensus. They would issue a statement through Mitch's office.

"Cool." Carlos winked at him. "I can sell my story to the tabloids and add on to the coffee house. I'll be set for life."

"You're already set for life. You have me," Abby said.

"You're right about that," he answered.

Jack caught Sally's gaze. "You raised a smart ass."

"Not really. He inherited sarcasm from you. I simply tutored him, honing his natural talent to what you see before you today."

"I'm so proud." He'd tried for a joking tone, but his ears told him he'd failed.

Carlos bowed from the waist, grinning. "It's all in the genes. I but useth my birthright to maketh my family proud."

Jack felt his pulse jump. Carlos joked, but this seemed like a real family moment. Coming together and facing difficulty, followed by laughter. Guess he should thank whoever leaked the story. Nah. They were still assholes.

"Anyone hungry? Want me to order a room service meal? Beer and wine are on ice. I asked Mitch to lay in your favorites. Should be veggies and fruit in the fridge."

Carlos took drink orders. Abby looked for the food, plates, and napkins. Sally watched them bustle, a melancholy look on her face.

He lifted his eyebrows and nodded at the empty space beside him on the couch. She slid next to him. Once he put his arm around her, pulling her closer, he knew he'd been given a precious gift. He hoped she hadn't changed her mind about sleeping with him. If she had, he'd make damn sure she reconsidered.

"They look good together, don't they?" he asked. "The way they work in sync, you'd think they'd been married for years."

Sally placed her hand on his chest, rubbing lightly. She snuggled closer. "I didn't think I'd ever say this to you, but you've been good for Carlos." She lowered her voice. "Good for me, too."

His pulse quickened. He whispered in her ear. "I'd make everything even better for you if you'd let me."

Her hand stilled. She lifted her chin and met his gaze. "Why don't we take life minute by minute, okay? We're here together. Let's enjoy our time."

He placed his hand over hers, pressing it against his chest. "My heart is yours."

"Thank you," she said, "for the precious gift."

He released her hand to take the beer Carlos offered. Sally's tremulous answer told him more than her words had. She cared for him. If he'd had an extra hand, he'd have made it into a fist and punched the sky.

They chatted about the concert. Sally related funny stories from the band's early days, when they'd played small gigs and weren't always appreciated. He'd forgotten many of the first jobs, and took her remembrances as another favorable sign that they could work out a future. Together.

The last time he'd been this contented had been when he and Sally were married. Barely keeping themselves in food and rent money but always finding laughter. And the night Carlos was born. Yep, that had left him feeling like he had the world by the ass.

He thought about the concerts playing to 50,000 or more fans. The first music awards they won. Going platinum. Those experiences kicked ass, but didn't compare to what was happening right here.

His son pulled Abby to her feet. "Looks like Dad is zoning out. What say, are you still wired or are you ready for bed?"

She yawned. "Bed. If I unwind anymore, there won't be much more than a single strand of me left to pick up."

Jack and Sally watched the young couple walk into their bedroom, their heads close together and arms entwined.

"They remind me so much of us," he said as he helped her stand. "I hope they have a better time of it than we did."

"That's the number one parental hope."

He pulled her into his arms. "I glanced over once

tonight, and you looked exactly the way you did when we met. Except for the dress and heels." He kissed the soft spot behind her ear. "I hope you never get rid of this outfit."

"What if I gain weight and the dress doesn't fit? What then?"

"I doubt that'll happen, but just pull it out of the closet. Don't even take the dress off the hanger. I'll get hard remembering how you looked tonight."

"Oh, Jack."

He laid down a string of kisses that ended at the corner of her mouth. About to capture the prize, she placed her finger over his lips.

"Wait, you only glanced over once? I must be losing my appeal." She batted her eyelashes. "I could have sworn you checked me out more often."

"You bet I did. And speaking of appeal, I'd love to peel our clothes off. Are you still—"

"Race you to the bedroom. Winner gets the top." She took two steps and stopped. "Aren't you going to race me?"

"Why spend energy running when I can use it to make us both happy."

She stood with her arms crossed, hip jutted to the side. "Right. You're afraid I'll win the race."

"I can't lose either way. But as long as you threw down a dare—" He drew her back to his chest. "I'll make sure we both win."

Chapter Sixteen

Sally didn't care that every stitch of clothing except her scarf had vanished quickly. Sure, she carried a few extra pounds, but the lights were dim, and her need to feel Jack's skin against hers took precedence.

She'd done a number on Jack's shirt—the buttons might land in the next state by morning. She remembered fumbling with Jack's zipper before he firmly pushed her hand aside and did it himself. The hot, open-mouthed kisses took her breath.

He pulled the scarf away from her throat in increments, his fingers and lips following the silken path. Then he matched their hands palm to palm and loosely wrapped the scarf around them. "This is a symbol to you. I won't leave you again, not in any lifetime."

"Do you know that you've basically hand fasted us?"

"No clue what that means and don't care what you call this." He motioned to their joined hands. "It's my promise."

He laid her on the bed and followed her down. Her glance moved to the side and stopped at the night table. Her muscles froze. There, nestled next to the table lamp, stood a familiar small plastic frame.

"I'd wondered what happened to that photo. Where did you? How?"

He followed her gaze. "I took it with me when I left on that first tour. I've carried that photograph with me on every tour. *Every* tour."

A hot, prickling sensation rested behind her eyes. She ran a finger over the frame and remembered when the picture was taken. The day she'd come home from the hospital with Carlos. Her younger self, holding their baby, looked into the camera eye, at Jack, with love.

Her finger outlined his lower lip. She struggled for words then abandoned the effort when he took her nipples one at a time into his mouth. Then he licked across them with one sweep, grinning at her after he finished. His grin slipped, and his free hand rested on her shoulder.

"I want honesty between us—no holding back this time. So you know...I've been tested. I'm clean."

She grew still, her one-handed grip on him tightening. "I haven't dated for a while. No tests, but no unprotected sex, either. Do you have a condom?"

"*A* condom? What makes you think I'm a one-trick pony?" He leaned away and caught her gaze. "Look, I've dated a bunch over the years—"

"Got remarried—"

"Yeah, took me awhile until I figured out I couldn't replace you. My heart wouldn't accept anyone else." He raised their bound wrists. "All that counts is right now."

Her heartbeat filled her ears, "now" echoing in her ears. She cleared her throat. "So are we going to talk or establish a personal best benchmark?"

The skin at the corner of Jack's eyes crinkled, his pupils expanded. "Hmm. Hard decision."

"If you're talking hard, I'd say, go for your

personal best. You're halfway there."

He ducked his head. "You should know not to challenge me." He licked and nipped his way from her neck to right under her breasts. "You never learn." His path moved toward her navel. "Looks like I'll have to prove my point."

A low moan ripped form Sally's throat. "Nuh uh."

"What? I didn't quite catch what you said."

"Together."

"Sorry. I need to set up the transition first before we sing the chorus."

She heard his low laugh right before feeling his fingers separate her curls then enter her wet inner self. Her body arched into the heel of his hand as her heels dug into the mattress.

"Sweet, so damn sweet." His hand continued to work on her while he returned his mouth to hers, their tongues lapping and tangling together.

Sally knew she was hotter than a fast food kitchen at noon. This is what desperation felt like, panting breaths included. "Can we get to the main attraction tonight or do I have to look for a younger man?" She writhed against him, tension building.

"I thought we could take the edge off with a quick—"

"No! You'll be too late."

"I love that arrogant professor speak." His fingers pulled out of her, his hand smoothed her curls. "Although, I haven't seen this side of you before. I should rethink—"

"You do and you'll find yourself in a coffin. I need you, *now*."

He moved over her, and she wrapped her legs

around his hips. She arched again, their bound hands at her shoulder.

She moaned. "Keep screwing around, and you'll miss my first orgasm."

"I can't miss out," he whispered, "but I need you around me again."

His slow, steady entry had her biting her lower lip to keep back another moan. He seated himself then pulled out, filling her repeatedly with long, lingering strokes.

She nipped at his earlobe then followed it up with a sucking kiss and their rhythm changed to a faster, harder one, pressure building with every stroke. She held onto Jack as if this physical union could erase their years apart.

"Babe, I've missed you."

She clutched him closer, unable to answer with words. Using her free hand she ran her fingers lightly over his buttocks and between them. She massaged the base of his spine then ran her hand back up to his shoulders.

Jack's panting changed to words. "Come with me."

"Always you. Only you."

Sweet tension increased until he tripped her trigger. With an upsurge, they erupted into a climax filled with color, light and music. Along with the orgasm she felt another sense; that of having reached home after an arduous journey.

****

Jack woke with Sally's arm splayed over his chest. One of her legs tangled with his. He inhaled the scent of warm woman, happy they'd found their way back to each other. Images of other mornings filled his thoughts as he watched her leave her dream world behind. She blinked awake.

"So, how do you feel after setting our benchmark?" Jack rubbed her ass, his half erection a pleasant, but not unexpected, reaction after the night they'd shared.

He followed the movement of her breasts as she stretched and yawned. Jumping out of bed for a quick shower was an over-rated idea when he had a soft handful nearby.

"Energized." She held her hand over her mouth. "In need of a toothbrush. Crap. I left my bag in the other bedroom."

"Use my brush." He raised his eyebrow at her wrinkled nose. "You're worried about sharing tooth germs? After the places our tongues were last night?"

She blushed. "Yeah, there is that." She slid her legs over the side of the bed, pulling the top sheet with her as she stood.

He grabbed the sheet, keeping her from covering herself. "Nope. That shy bullshit doesn't work for me. I want to see you, all of you, in the morning light."

She opened and closed her mouth without speaking.

He pushed the comforter aside and pointed to himself. "This body has seen some miles, Sally. I'm no prize, with a bad back and assorted pains." He smacked his lips. "And morning breath."

Ignoring a back twinge, he pulled her into his arms. "But you. God, you're just as I remember. My Morning Goddess."

Her shining eyes told him she'd remembered his endearment, voiced every morning they were together.

"I want to wake up every morning next to my

goddess. What do you say?"

Her body stiffened under his hands.

"I, um, I love you Jack."

She didn't continue, so he voiced the word he knew hovered between them. "But?"

"I've enjoyed knowing you again, our dinners, daily talks, and shared history."

"And the sex." He pulled back. "Don't tell me you faked multiple orgasms. You aren't an actress. Or a star fucker."

She grinned. "Sex with you is plenty hot without the added celebrity status."

"I repeat. But?"

She inhaled through her nose. "But. We don't have the same beliefs. Helping people in my store, meditation, discovering new philosophies, all of that, is who I am."

"I get that. I'm not asking you to change. We're not so different."

"Sure we are. Besides being rich and famous, you think metaphysics is crap." She shook her finger at him. "That's a direct quote."

He grasped her finger and brought it to his mouth. As he sucked, her pupils darkened. Pulling her finger free with a pop, he nuzzled her temple.

"I believe in tantric sex with the woman I love. I believe that music has magical power, could even be the basis of the universe." He placed his palms on her jaw and lowered his lips to hers. "I believe most in the music we make together. How can that not work for you?"

Their kiss deepened, interrupted by a back spasm that left Jack hunched in pain.

"Shit. Damned back. Shit."

Sally helped him to the bed. She rubbed her palms together with quick motions. "Jack, do I have your permission to use energy work on you?"

He gasped a breath. "Crap. Do whatever it is you do. I can't hurt any more."

"No, but you can hurt less."

"Sorry. Bad spasm."

He closed his eyes against the sight of Sally waving her hands over his body. As he replayed the scene, he recognized that she used specific movements that seemed to push and pull the air above his body. Spasms racked him again, but less strong this time.

A quiet, one of bone deep peace he hadn't experienced in the years without Sally, slowly filled his mind. Rippling spasms moved down his back and disappeared. He gave himself over to the peaceful feeling flooding him.

Jack woke to Sally's hand pressing on his shoulder. "How are you feeling?"

He took stock. "No spasms. Good. I feel good." He covered her hand and squeezed. "Thank you. I don't know what you did, but it worked." He rubbed his finger over his lips. "What you did…didn't hurt you, did it?"

"You're welcome and no, I don't take on the negative energy." She sank down beside his hip. "Do you see now? I can help people and make a difference. I can't give that up." She handed him a glass of water. "You need to hydrate."

He sat up and drank. "You're being stubborn. We can find a way to mesh our lives. All we need is love."

She shook her head. "Don't go quoting lyrics at

me. This whole thing with Carlos and the media scares me."

He wasn't so cocksure about their chances at privacy, but he knew she needed reassurance. "One hit wonder, babe. We'll send out a statement, the press will kick the story around for a day or two, then it'll all end."

"I have a bad feeling about this."

He rubbed his chest. "Shit. I hope you're wrong."

"You mean you believe me?"

"I should have listened to you about coming to Charlotte. I thought I could control the scene. Instead, I screwed up."

"Words of love, Jack. You're singing a seductive tune."

"I do my best. Let me play you the refrain." He palmed the back of her head and captured her mouth. He pulled away, his lips hovering above hers. "Together, we're invincible, babe."

A sharp knock sounded.

"It's me," Carlos said through the door. "Don't want to interrupt, but I think you should turn on Channel Four. Or Channel Seven. Or any channel. Dad's face is everywhere."

Chapter Seventeen

Sally scrambled for the remote, but Jack beat her to it and flipped on the set. A young blonde woman's face filled the screen. The sound cut on in mid-sentence.

"Although Glynnis McKinney did not leave with Jack Reed, sources tell us they were seen in a hot embrace before the show. Are the birth parents of Rough Cuts drummer Tony Shaw's adopted daughter Cristal reuniting? And how does the previously unknown son fit into the picture? Diamond Jack left by another door in an effort to avoid reporters on the scene." The picture cut to a shot of their limousine driving off, followed by the SUV.

"Jack Reed is uncommunicative. Calls to the Rough Cuts manager, Stuart Mitchell, were also not returned. We'll keep you posted on this fast-breaking story."

She collapsed against the headboard, her thoughts spinning. This was worse than she anticipated. The upside was that she could once again clearly see auras. Having sex with Jack seemed to have been the key. The downside was the colors around Jack were murky and dark instead of clear and bright.

"Shit. Fuck. Piss. This sucks." Jack spat the words. "Figures that bitch Glynnis would find a way to get some air time for herself." He pulled on his jeans.

"Are you planning to confront the media while

going commando?"

"Fuck the media. Carlos and Abby come first. Then our shower."

She had already pulled on a hotel bathrobe and smoothed her hair behind her shoulders. Grabbing his hand, she stopped him before he pulled on a T-shirt. "Slow down. Take a deep breath. Now take two more." His chest rose and fell in long inhalations. His face regained color.

"Crisis response works better with a calm mind." She patted his arm. "Now we'll be better armed to face the problem."

He pulled her in to a hug. "See? This is why I need you around."

"If I weren't here, the story about Carlos would be nonexistent. Plus, I remember that you never got upset about people's comments when they concerned you. You only flew off the handle when someone was unkind to a person you cared about." She smoothed her hand over his chest. "We knew what could happen and chose *you*."

"Damn, woman."

"Let's see how the kids want to handle this. Then I've got some serious shower work in mind." Jack's color looked better, but she sensed he had some residual back pain. Hot water would complete the cure.

They entered the suite's living room hand in hand. Carlos and Abby sat at the table drinking coffee. An array of dishes, some covered, filled the surface.

"Hey Mom. Dad," Carlos said. "Sorry to roust you, but I figured the sooner you knew about the story, the better." His tone was casual, but the set of his shoulders gave away his stress.

Jack pulled out her chair then moved his closer to her. His thigh pressed against hers. No sense pretending they hadn't shared a bed last night. She laced her fingers with Jack's and caught her son's eye.

"Sweetie, what's your take? Do you want to go ahead with the statement we drafted last night, or take another direction?"

He pinned Jack with a glare. "First I want to know the truth about Glynnis. Are you playing my mom?"

"Son, you were with me almost all night. What do you think?"

Carlos glanced between Jack and Sally. "Stupid question."

"Thanks for sticking up for me, sweetie. Now let's decide about the statement." Sally's heart warmed. She'd never worry about how she'd raised Carlos again. True he hadn't had the financial advantages he could have experienced, but he'd learned how to be a decent human.

"Abby and I think that's still our best option. We'll get Mitch's office to fine tune our words and ask for privacy."

Jack nodded. "Sounds like a plan."

She tapped her fingers against her cup. "Any takers on odds the media will respect our request?"

Jack snorted. "Sucker bet." He rubbed his forehead with his free hand. "Shit. I'm sorry I dragged you all into this mess."

She covered their entwined hands with her other palm. "Enough guilt, already. We're adults. We can deal." Her gaze took in the kids. "The dogs are settled, right? What about the café? And your mural work?"

"Already handled," her son said. "Abby has one

small job with a flexible completion date, and I called my employees. They're happy to step in until this blows over. I told them to bring in whoever they needed to help cover."

Another wave of pride filled her. Until Abby, Carlos had never stepped away from his business, even though he had a crackerjack crew. He'd learned to let go, thanks to her.

"I can't figure out who leaked the story," Abby said. "Everyone we met last night is devoted to the band. No one in that group would want to hurt you, Jack."

"Well, there is Glynnis," Sally said.

Jack sighed. "I thought of her too, except—"

"Except what?"

"One of the reporters in the press conference asked some pointed questions. The conference took place before Glynnis showed, I think. That tells me someone inside talked." His lips thinned. "I'm hoping it wasn't crew, but we had to take on some new roadies and security this trip. Some of our regular guys weren't expecting a tour and weren't available."

He caught Abby's eye. "I hate to burst your bubble, but not everyone is loyal when it comes to money."

Sally listened for answers from her spirit guides, but they weren't talking. She also couldn't see auras, though she figured they'd be a chaotic mess.

"Mitch will find out," Jack said. "The man has ears everywhere."

She received a sudden picture of blue jeans, a uniform, and an image of a silk blouse.

"What do you think, Sally?" Jack tapped her hand. "Your spidey sense providing any answers?"

He wasn't teasing. He really asked. A flash of euphoria swept her.

"I think three people were involved, a tech or roadie, one of the security guards, and Glynnis. I don't know how it played out, but that's what I'm seeing."

"I believe you," he said. He sipped his coffee. "I'll e-mail the draft to Mitch and give him your leads, then we can grab a shower."

She squeezed his hand. "Let's eat first."

He grinned. "You're right. I'd better build up my strength. Who knows what could happen in that seven-jet shower."

Her face heated.

"Hey you guys," Carlos said. "I wanted my parents to get along not embarrass me with their sexual prowess."

"Think of it this way, son. You've inherited kick ass genes that will allow you to get it on with Abby for many years."

Carlos put his arm around Abby. "I think we can both get behind that."

****

Jack pulled Sally under the spray. "Did you notice the shower seat? I can make love with you and not have to worry about throwing my back out."

"Nothing I appreciate more than an intelligent lover."

Water sluiced over their shoulders and between them, beating away residual aches from their previous night's activities. They soaped and rinsed, tried the shower seat then decided they preferred the bed.

"Good thing the hotel has a large hot water supply," Jack said. He shook his head, water flying from his hair.

She passed him a fluffy bath sheet. "I agree. I've stayed in some hotels where, if you didn't get an early shower, you had to wait until mid-morning for hot water."

His blood pressure spiked. He worked to keep his tone even. "Where was this? Some lover too cheap to treat you as you deserve?"

She stopped patting herself dry. "Don't tell me you're jealous. You? Mr. Flick-A-Wrist-Get-A-Woman?"

He buried his face in his towel.

"Don't think you can pretend to dry yourself and avoid answering."

"Okay, yeah, I'm jealous, but I'm more pissed. You deserve the best of everything, not some half-assed hotel that can't provide enough hot water."

Her face held no expression, and then she smiled, lightening his heart. "Not a lover, a college-funded trip to a seminar. Blue Peak College isn't Ivy League." She pulled his towel from him. "But I think your defense of me is sweet."

"Sweet? Is that all? I was hoping for gratitude."

"Thanks, sweetie."

He held her face between his palms. "More tangible gratitude." His voice turned gravely. "Physical. Gratitude."

She went up on tiptoes and gave him a peck on the cheek.

"I can see the professor needs a seminar."

She lightly slapped his bare chest. "And I can see keeping your ego in check is a full-time job."

"You can handle it."

They kissed their way to the rumpled bed.

"I scanned the concert review that Carlos earmarked," she said. "They claimed you'd never played better. As if you were exorcising demons in the second half. Musical history."

"Babe, did you write that review? Yeah, I was working out my guilt about Billy, but I played my best because my family was there." His hand snaked out and encased her breast. "I didn't want to let anyone down. Especially not you."

He pushed his growing erection into her hip.

"Feels like you don't want to let me down this morning, either."

"Honey, I can't help myself." His hand moved down to rub her stomach. "By the way, did I tell you to never get rid of that black dress?"

She licked the sensitive area behind his ear. "Yeah. Are you wanting me to wear it again?"

He moaned as her hands slipped down his sides to rest at his hips, fingers circling.

She threw a leg across his waist. "I don't mind putting it on if you're planning to undress…me."

He put his hands on her waist and rolled her on her back. "Maybe later."

\*\*\*\*

Abby leaned closer with an innocent look on her face. "So, Sally, are you enjoying getting to know Jack?"

She laughed. "You are merciless."

Abby smoothed down the front of her shirt with the palm of her hand. "I know. I learned from you."

"How is Carlos handling this mess? Really?"

"He's fine. Really."

"You're caught up in this, too. Your lovely private wedding is looking less likely." She slapped her hand over her mouth. "I take that back. I don't want that negative stuff coming true. Your wedding will be as you wished."

"Not exactly."

She leaned forward. "What are you saying, Abby? You're still being married, aren't you? Please don't leave Carlos."

"Oh for goodness sake. Calm down. Your son is not getting away from me again. No, I'm sorry to say my mother called earlier."

"Oh, joy. Sorry. What did she say?"

"For starters, that she was horrified, simply beside herself to learn I was engaged to the son of a dirty musician."

"Hey, that's not fair. Jack takes showers. I helped wash him myself not long ago." She waved her hand as if shooing a fly. "Oops. Too much information. What other gems did she disperse?"

"I can't believe your proposed father-in-law is a man they're saying fathered a child out of wedlock, then paid his friend to adopt. Goodness knows how he treated that son of his." She dropped her mimicking voice. "She thinks Jack uses drugs without stop, even though he only had two beers during our dinner. Well, he did call her Marge. Did you tell him to do that?"

"No, Jack figured her out all on his own. Come on, tell me the rest. You need to get this out."

"She threw out a few more insults against Jack, including the idea that he breaks every traffic law for fun, specifically speeding through school zones."

"I'll say it again. How you turned out as sweet as

you have with…never mind. I'm sure there's more."

"She wants me to break the engagement immediately."

"Or?"

"Or she'll leave for home and boycott the wedding. She implied she'd disown me."

"So you must choose between your mother and Carlos?"

Abby nodded. "Yep. "

She tapped her finger against her chin. "I have an idea that may turn her around. Give her time to calm down. She won't believe the stories are lies, but ask her to ignore the news."

"What will you do?"

"That's easy. Appeal to her snobbery." And her need for attention.

What she wouldn't tell Abby is that she'd have to ask Jack's mother for help. The same woman who hadn't lifted a finger to see Carlos, but who now professed to care for him. The last time she'd seen Eleanor Young, she'd been offered a free makeover. Her then mother-in-law had made no secret that she thought Jack should have married someone from the privileged social set.

On the other hand, Carlos and Abby had exclaimed over Eleanor's warmth and generosity when they'd visited. Abby had described the touching reunion between grandmother and grandson. Her picture of the event had portrayed a different woman than the one populating Sally's memory banks.

Sometimes letting go of the past hurt, and the process always meant looking at your own part in the drama. Back in the day, she couldn't have changed any more than the Young family. For her son and Abby's sakes, she'd take the first step. That meant calling Eleanor directly.

The things she did for love.

Chapter Eighteen

"Eleanor, this is Sally, Sally Ford. In case you don't remember me, I'm your grandson's mother."

"Hello, dear. I'm so glad you called."

Sally stared at her phone, checking the number she'd dialed.

"Sally?"

She replaced the receiver to her ear. "Yes, I'm sorry. I thought perhaps I had the wrong number."

Eleanor laughed. "It's been a long time since I offered to buy you clothes and cosmetics."

Now why had she mentioned the one memory guaranteed to hurt? Had she not changed much, after all?

"I must apologize for that thoughtless act, dear." A sigh sounded over the line. "I won't blame my husband for my words, but he certainly ruled the roost back then. And I allowed him the power. I am so sorry that I hurt you. I knew I had at the time, but I really had no idea how to communicate with you. We inhabited different social worlds."

Sally's chest hurt. The woman's words seemed meant to soothe but still held a bite.

"That era held so much upheaval. Your world was bright, filled with opportunity and creativity. The future waited for you. My existence was closed off, rigid and dominated with men who told me how to act. I think, yes, I believe I was jealous of you. Oh, not because you'd married my son, but because you had a freedom I couldn't imagine."

"Is that why you supported your husband when he manufactured a divorce?"

"Dear, we're both older now. I can't change my actions, but I can apologize. Will you accept my regrets? You did a wonderful job raising Carlos. Had my husband taken a hand in his education, well, who knows."

Sally's thoughts whirled. She hadn't expected apologies and explanations when she'd called. Although she couldn't see Eleanor, her intuition told her past hurts and anger had no part in this conversation. Still, the familiar complaints were hard to release.

"Dear, I'm so happy that Carlos called looking for his father. I can't tell you what a difference knowing him has meant for me. And Jack, of course. He was not a happy man until Carlos contacted him. Now he sounds at ease with the world."

"I'm glad that you accepted Carlos and welcomed both he and Abby into the fold."

"You mean, more than I welcomed you?"

"Lay it on the line, why don't you."

"My health is improved in the last few years, but I'm not so foolish as to believe I'll live forever."

The words hit Sally in her solar plexus.

"I know we've had a difficult history, dear. But I hope you will consider granting me my fondest wish."

"I'm not sure I can help you."

"Allow an old woman her fantasies, will you? My desire is the same one you share. To see my son settled happily with the woman he loves. I already have a grandchild, and I'm sure you'll have one of your own. You see, we share more than you think. We share a love for Jack, isn't that right?"

Sally swallowed hard. "Sometimes even love isn't enough."

"Oh, pish. Love is the strongest force on Earth, and you know it. But love can't get a foothold in a closed heart. I'm hoping you'll let his love for you become part of your life. If you would, you'd make my dream for my son come true."

A chill traveled her spine. Given what she now knew about Jack's world, she wasn't sure she could offer him enough love. No time to think about how to work out their lives. "You always did play hardball."

"That wasn't me, my dear, that was my husband and his father." She cleared her throat. "Of course, I did pick up several strategies from them over the years."

"I suspect there is more to you than anyone has ever known."

"I'll tell you all my secrets if you give my boy another chance."

"I, uh—" She tamped down her instinctive distrust of the Young family. "Thank you, Eleanor. I appreciate your saying these things to me."

"I would have said them much sooner, had we had the opportunity to speak. I'm glad to finally get this off my chest. Life is too short to carry hate and regrets, don't you think?"

"Yes, I do." Suddenly, using Eleanor to put Margaret down made her cringe.

"Is there something I can do for you? Or did you call to reestablish contact before the wedding?"

"I, uh—"

"Don't prevaricate with me, Sally. If we're to be friends, we must be honest. What is the problem? Do you need help with the wedding? I understood from Carlos that everything is under control."

*From Carlos?*

"Such a sweet man, my grandson. You do know he visited with Abby? We had such a lovely time together. He and Abby call regularly. I'll do anything I can to ensure their wedding goes off without a hitch."

Her last sentence made Sally's decision easier. "Actually, that's why I called."

"Abby's mother is causing problems, isn't she? Sounds like a trumped up bit of work. Well? Are you going to tell me what's going on, or shall I call my grandson?"

That's what she loved about elders. You could hear humble apologies then watch them mount their high horse the next second. Eleanor's sense of propriety hadn't lessened, but neither had she feigned her willingness to fight for family.

"We need you to fix this situation. Here's what's happened so far." Sally filled her in on her conversation with Abby.

"I've never seen a couple more in love. Those two belong together."

Her past hurts reminded her Eleanor hadn't thought the same of her son and his wife. First wife.

Eleanor's next words spoke directly to Sally's thoughts. "I can't say we were wrong to break you and Jack apart. I saw attraction and affection between you, but not the commitment."

Her anger rose quickly and as rapidly cooled with

recognition of the truth. "I know, and you're right."

"People grow, don't they?"

"With luck and work, yes."

"I never thought I'd say this, Sally, but you and my son, I believe you belong together now. Give him the opportunity to show himself to you. He needs you."

She brushed at her chest, her heart a mass of conflicting emotion. "I understand."

"Do you? Leaving him now, when the media is on him like a hound pack to a fox, would inflict lasting damage. I don't think I'm being dramatic when I say he wouldn't recover emotionally. We mothers, we know these things."

Of all things, she'd trumped Sally with the mother card.

"You don't need to use the Liberty Bell to hit me over the head."

"No? I seem to recall you were quite stubborn," Eleanor said.

"I don't like to feel pushed into decisions."

"We can agree on that. Now, what will we do to help Abby?"

After a short discussion, Eleanor agreed to handle Margaret. Sally ended the call and stepped into the suite's living room. The large area was flooded with sunlight. Jack perched on the end of a couch, plucking out a series of chords. She saw the notebook beside him and recognized he worked on a new song. He'd always been able to turn his experiences into a melody and lyrics that spoke to everyone who'd gone through similar events. She'd found peace through meditation. Beliefs and practices didn't matter as much as growing and adapting the best you could.

He looked up but continued strumming. "Hey, babe."

"Keep working. I didn't mean to interrupt."

"Nah, I've got the major idea nailed down." He swung his guitar onto the couch next to him and stood. "I'd ask if you wanted to use the pool or go down for lunch, but Mitch says to sit tight." He moved his head from side to side. "Don't know why, but that makes me want to go somewhere."

"You always were a rebel."

"Yeah. You too. Who'd have thought Carlos would turn out as he did?"

"Not me, though he reminded me of you more often than I liked."

Jack raised his eyebrows.

"Practical, focused on what he wanted, stubborn."

"Nuh, uh, that stubborn part is you."

Her lips quirked. "Then I'll say he's persistent. Sound familiar?"

"Okay, fine, he got a dose of stubborn from both of us. Didn't seem to hurt him any." He pulled her against his chest. "If stubborn will get me more time with you, I'll dig my heels in right now. I want you, more than I can say, sing, play, anything." He lowered his head and murmured against her lips. "I hope you'll stick with me. For the rest of our days together."

Sally wondered at his comment. She'd heard basically the same worry from Eleanor a few minutes earlier. What had Jack told his mother? And why did they both think she'd flip out and leave? She'd never thought herself a quitter.

Jack deepened the kiss. She tightened her arms around his waist, her worries drifting away on a rising tide of warmth and sensuality.

"Ah, geez. Guess I need to learn to knock."

They'd been too involved to hear the lock click. Jack's lips turned up in a smile, but he didn't pull away. Sally ended the kiss but couldn't move from his tight embrace.

"Hi, sweetie," she said. "You didn't leave the floor, did you?"

"Abby and I were getting to know Cristal. Abby is still down the hall." He ran his fingers through his hair. "Women aren't all that subtle when they want to talk female stuff, so I came back here. I'll hang in our bedroom." He grinned. "I'll turn the television up loud, so don't worry about making noise out here." He shook his head. "I knew I'd have to warn my kids about making noise, but not my parents."

Sally pulled away from Jack. "I should call the store. You guys can hang together."

"I'm waiting for your answer on sticking," Jack said.

She avoided his gaze. "We'll talk. Promise. I'll be right back."

**\*\*\*\***

Jack watched Sally walk into their room. Why the hell did he never get a break with her? Every time it looked like they'd win, life happened.

"So. You and Mom?"

He glanced at his son. "She's keeping me waiting."

"Nah," Carlos said. "She's made up her mind, but she won't admit it. Stubborn to a fault, that's Mom."

"You know this, how?"

"She wouldn't have slept with you if she weren't ready to commit." His face scrunched. "Yew. Did I just say that about my mother?"

Their glances met and laughter bubbled up. Carlos's expression sobered.

"I have to admit, having parents who get along has been my dream. The possibility of that dream coming true means more now, with Abby's mother flipping out."

A chill traveled his body. "Tell me." He listened to his son's report with growing anger. "What a bitch."

"You're referring to my future relation, but yeah. She's got some screwed up notion about status and reputation."

He rubbed his forehead. What the hell else would get cocked up because of his re-entry into his son's life? He should have rebuffed Carlos at the first phone call, or kept his distance at minimum, but the lure of finally knowing his son had been too great.

He'd put off telling Carlos about the investigator's reports because he'd wanted to talk in person, not over the phone. Confessing when they'd been out West together would have been a good time, but he hadn't wanted to jeopardize their early relationship. He still worried Carlos would think him a loser or sick stalker. Time he knew what Jack had done.

On the other hand, Sally could easily cut off his balls, make them into pate. and serve them back on rustic bread she'd baked fresh. Her privacy had always been important to her, and knowing a stranger had reported on Carlos's life would send her into a temper he didn't want to experience firsthand. Not that he'd have a choice, now. Screaming headlines threatened everything they could become. Fuck.

"I'll call my mother," Jack said.

"No need. I spoke with her earlier." Sally returned to his side.

He couldn't read her expression, but her color was high.

"She's agreed to contact Abby's mother. I suspect Marge's protest about the wedding will disappear once those two are through talking."

"Great." He inhaled but couldn't catch his breath. "Look, I need to tell you both something." His ex-wife and son moved closer.

"What's wrong?" Sally asked.

"Do you want us to leave? We've caused you problems, haven't we?" Carlos's expression caught him in the chest.

"What? Christ, no. The thought of you coming to see me here made the rest of the tour bearable." He shook his head. "Balls. That's not nearly honest enough." He pulled them into a three-way hug. "Now that I have you back, I can't face living without you."

He hung onto them knowing the secret he had to reveal would change how they viewed him, perhaps drive one or both of them away. On the other hand, he might get lucky, and they'd see his actions for what they were: desperate attempts to be involved with his child the only way he could, from a distance.

They broke from the hug but remained standing close together. He leaned to inhale the scent of Sally's freshly shampooed hair, brushed his palm over the silky tresses. "What I did well, I thought it was for love. You may think otherwise. Know this." He caught their gaze one by one. "I never meant to hurt you."

"What the hell, Dad. You're scaring me. Tell us already. Waiting sucks."

The corner of his mouth kicked up. "Yeah, you got that right." He motioned to the seating area. "Let's sit down."

Abby burst through the door. "You have to do something, Jack. Those sleaze balls are going after Cristal."

He stilled. "Tell me."

"We went down to the exercise room." She held up her hand. "I know we shouldn't have, but we figured no one would bother us. We're not you or the other guys in the band, Jack."

He noted and then ignored his increased pulse rate. "What. Happened."

"We were using the treadmills when a reporter came in."

"You need a room key to enter, so how'd he get in?" Carlos asked.

Jack already knew the answer. "He slipped someone on staff money. Where is Cristal now?"

"I left her behind and ran to get the manager's help."

"Son-of-a...I'd better go down and get her," Jack said.

Sally placed her hand on his arm in a staying motion. "I'll go. No one knows me, and while I'm down there, I'll speak to the manager about his staff."

"Rip him a new one for me, babe," Jack said.

She nodded and hurried from the room. Jack watched the door slam shut then put it on the latch. "She forgot her key," he said as he rejoined them. "Now, let's sit down, Abby, and you can tell me what you heard."

He noted her hands shook until Carlos put his arm

around her and pulled her close.

"The guy asked if she knew her mother's whereabouts. No, wait, he mentioned Glynnis's name. When Cristal said she had no idea, the reporter asked what she thought about being your daughter but shuttled off in adoption to your friend."

Jack snarled a curse. "Anything else?"

She nodded. "Yes, he wanted to know how she felt about meeting her long-lost brother." Abby moved closer to Carlos on the facing loveseat. "That's when I ran to the manager and came back." She leaned forward. "Jack, I'm sorry. We never should have left the floor."

He dredged up a smile. "Not your fault." He sighed. "I guess I was right to leave all those years ago."

She straightened. "Jack, no."

Carlos leaned forward. "Dad, that's bullshit. The past is gone." He gripped Abby's hand. "But I do want to know what you were about to tell Mom and I before the interruption. Unless you want to wait until she returns?"

He ran his fingers through his hair. "I should probably hold off, but I think I've waited too long already."

"Geez, Dad, you look like the world is ending." He rubbed his chin. "Does this have to do with Cristal?"

"No." He took a deep breath. "Shit, there's no easy way to tell this. I, um, I wanted to know you were doing okay. That you were safe after your mother divorced…I mean after we split." He rubbed the nape of his neck. "Yeah, so um, I hired a private investigator and got regular reports, photos."

"I see," Carlos replied.

"You see what?" Jack asked. "That I was a gutless wonder? Hiring someone to check on you when I should have done that myself?"

"Crap, Dad. You really need to do something about that guilt complex you haul around in a tractor-trailer behind you."

"Huh?" He stared at his son. "You mean you're not pissed?"

Carlos shook his head. "Nana Young told me. I've seen the photos and reports. I saw that photo of you sitting in the bleachers during one of my swim meets."

"Yeah, well, more than one meet. I was there when your team won State Championship. I couldn't, you know—"

"I do know. Threw me off at first, but I understand your motives now. I'd probably do the same thing." Carlos hugged Abby. "Not that you'll have a chance to turn my very smart fiancée against me the way your father worked on you."

"Wouldn't think of it."

"One thing. You need to tell Mom, sooner than later."

Jack's stomach dropped. "I know. Want to run interference for me?"

Carlos shook his head. "No way."

They shared a grin, but Jack's stomach muscles cramped. He'd stop procrastinating and tell Sally as soon as she returned.

"Dad, is Cristal my sister? Half-sister."

"Yeah, Jack, it's time you told the truth." Cristal stood in the doorway with her hands on her hips. "The whole truth for a change."

"But not with the door open," Sally said. She settled next to Jack on the couch. "By the time I arrived, the reporter had left. The manager escorted us back." She nodded. "Yes, he was walking funny by the time I finished with him."

"Good." He focused on Cristal seated in the chair next to him. "Are you okay?"

She grinned. "Are you kidding? Watching Sally was a tutorial in telling someone off while making them almost enjoy the process. The manager would have jumped from the moving elevator if he could have found a way out."

His muscles loosened. "She *was* a professor, you know."

Cristal swung her legs over the chair's arm. "Is Sally as proud of that fact as you are?" She stretched her arms. "The worst part was not getting to finish my workout." She looked to Abby. "We were having a great talk."

Abby nodded and winked, then glanced between Sally and Jack.

He wouldn't ask about the wink. Some things were better left unknown. "Did the reporter give you his name? I'll have him barred from the concert tonight. If he shows, and I figure he will."

Cristal shook her finger at him. "More important is telling Carlos the truth."

He didn't need to examine his son's expression to know she was right. "Yeah, well, you may not be too pleased with your old man once I tell you the story."

Sally snorted. "We had this discussion last night. Not. Your. Fault."

He nodded then caught Carlos's eye. "Here goes."

After relaying an abbreviated version he awaited his son's verdict.

"Damn, too bad. I'd have liked a sister. I get your protecting Cristal and Billy. That's pure you." He tilted his head. "I kind of figured she wasn't related though, given the family genes are so strong."

That was it? No recriminations? He'd really lucked out in the progeny department.

"Besides not looking a lick like Jack, I'd rather play with a soundboard than a musical instrument," Cristal said. "I'm sick of the rumors, though. You wouldn't believe the people who've sucked up to me only because they think I'm related to Diamond Jack Reed."

"How sad you had those experiences," Sally said.

Jack's pulse drummed. Was she preparing to say, "I told you so?"

"You had a lot to learn, and it's made you stronger. You are an amazing young woman, one I'm proud to know." She cleared her throat. "How should we proceed? Are there steps we can take to ensure our privacy?"

Jack shook his head. "Mitch is already working on the problem. Let's see what he recommends." He wished he could ensure continued secrecy but knew that option had passed.

"Well, I know what I'm going to do," Cristal said. "I'd bet my new lap top that Glynnis has got something to do with these rumors. Why else would the reporter ask her location?"

Jack had the same thought, and so did the others if their expressions were an indication. He frowned. "What are you planning?"

"Glynnis may be my birth mother, but I won't let her use me." She caught Jack's eye. "She's counted on you and Tony protecting me. Time I did something about that." She jumped to her feet and strode out before anyone glimpsed her intention.

Jack moved to stand, but Sally restrained him. "No, let her go. She's an adult, and experienced beyond her years."

"But cutting off her birth mother?" Carlos leaned forward and hung his hands between his knees. "At least Glynnis remembered Cristal's birthdays, even if she sucked air the rest of the year."

Silence fell over the room.

"Sorry, Dad. I didn't mean—"

Jack held up a hand, palm out. "No, don't apologize. I screwed up."

Sally put her arm around his waist. "I screwed up, too. I thought…Carlos, I believed you would be hurt due to Jack's growing notoriety. Now that I've met Cristal, I understand I didn't give either you or your father credit for having a brain. Anger makes people do stupid things. So does fear. Sweetie, I deliberately kept Jack from you. I told myself I'd acted in your best interest, but that's not true." She kept her arm around Jack's waist and leaned against him.

"Oh, shit," Carlos said. "Neither of you had much of a choice when my grandfathers got involved. Grandmother Young told me all about the finagled divorce. Those two old coots knew exactly how to play both of you." He glanced between them. "We talked for hours. I saw photographs." Carlos raised his eyebrows as if sending a message to him.

Jack stiffened. His momentum for raising the

private investigator topic with Sally had been broken with Abby's interruption. Hell, there would be no perfect time. May as well dive in right now.

"Hey, Jack." Tony pounded on the door. "Are you in there?"

He moved to admit his friend. Tony pushed past Jack and turned to face him with his fists on his hips.

"What the hell, man. Siccing the press on Cristal?" He shook his head. "Dickhead."

Jack raised his hands in a surrender pose. "Not me."

"Well, fuck me. Some reporter is claiming an exclusive story. Promises film."

Sally rose. "Cristal said she was going to straighten out her birth mother."

"Shit." Jack's nape hair stood on end. "No, she said she was going to do something about the stories. She said we'd protected her long enough."

He exchanged a quick glance with Tony. They headed for the door. "Find out if Mitch is in the building," Jack yelled over his shoulder. "Tell him Cristal needs help."

"Where is she?" Abby called.

"With a freaking reporter. Tell him to check the lobby, dining room, and cocktail lounge. I doubt she'd go far and that dipshit reporter was likely waiting right outside."

The two friends moved through the door and toward the elevator at a run.

"I can't believe that kid of mine," Tony said.

"I can. She's got more guts than sense. Like you."

Tony jammed the elevator call button. "Jealous?"

Jack added several frustrated button pushes of his

own. "Nope. I've got my own dynamite primed."

They exchanged long looks and pushed into the elevator car before the doors had finished opening.

Chapter Nineteen

Jack pulled in a quick breath. Cristal and the reporter who'd asked the pointed questions at the press conference sat together at a small table in a deserted cocktail lounge. A cameraman waited to the side, lights off.

He grabbed Tony's shoulder to gain his attention. "You think we're too late?"

Tony shrugged.

Cristal stood as they gained the table. "Dad. I can handle this."

Tony stuck his hands in his front pockets. "Not saying you can't. We're here as back-up." He leaned back on his heels. His eyes narrowed. "Nobody hassles my little girl."

"Da-ad. I arranged the interview, okay? It's way past time to stop the gossip."

They locked gazes. "You know some people still think the moon shot was faked, right?"

"Yeah," she said. "And Elvis, JFK, and Jim Morrison are alive."

He nodded, his lips curving up. "That's my girl."

Jack slid into a chair at the adjoining table. His back muscles were tight, on the verge of spasms. He knew Cristal was right, but wished she'd chosen another path.

The reporter fidgeted. "So are you ready to make

your statement on the record? We'd like to get back in time for the noon slot."

She smiled. "I know about timing. And you won't hesitate to use what I told you off record. I'm not a dumb kid. I saw the record light glowing on the camera. Yeah, start filming."

The reporter gestured to his cameraman, and bright lights flicked on.

She looked directly into the camera lens. "I'm Cristal Shaw, my dad is Tony Shaw of The Rough Cuts. For years, people have gossiped that I'm really Jack's Reed's daughter. I'm here to tell you the truth."

Jack admired the slight pause she took. No one could bash her poise or timing.

"My birth mother named Jack Reed in a bogus paternity suit for revenge. Medical reports prove my father was Billy Hatter, a member of the Cuts' technical crew who died before I was born. Jack has kept quiet even when reporters continued printing unsubstantiated rumors as truth." She turned her gaze to Jack and the camera followed. "He's one of my favorite people, but he's not, and never will be, my father."

Standing, she moved to crouch next to Tony. "Tony Shaw and his wife Liz are the best parents on the planet." She kissed him on the cheek. He slung his arm over her shoulders. "Jack Reed didn't pay anyone to adopt me. Tony and Liz, my real mom and dad, gave me a life I never would have had without them."

She rose and laid her hand on Tony's shoulder. "I know some of you are disappointed in the truth, but that's all I have for you. Thanks for listening." Cristal made the universal finger across the neck gesture.

The camera lights died.

The reporter checked his watch. He caught Jack's eye then Tony's. "So now that Cristal has set the record straight, how about you two? We could put off the report for the evening news."

Tony grabbed Cristal in a tight hug. "My girl said it all better than I could."

"Jack?" The reporter picked up his pen. "Want to address the recent statement regarding your son? The person you've never acknowledged before now? And what about Glynnis McKinney? You getting back with her? The photos of you two kissing are pretty steamy."

He fought to keep a straight face as a spasm wracked his lower back. He lowered his head as the camera lights lit up the table in front of him. Breathing through his nose, he fought the waves of pain.

Tony moved to block the camera. Cristal positioned herself next to him.

"I asked you here to make my story public, not to ambush Jack," Cristal said. "He's already made his statement and asked for privacy. You'd better leave or you'll miss your noon slot."

The room darkened, and chairs scraping against tile floors filled Jack's hearing. He breathed through his nose, willing away the last of the spasms.

A business card appeared on the table before him. "Let me know when you're ready to talk, Jack. I promise to go easy on you."

He didn't, couldn't move as another spasm hit. He white knuckled the chair arms after Tony guided the two newsmen away.

Cristal placed her mouth next to his ear. "Jack, are you okay?"

He gave one short nod.

"Geez, I'm sorry, Jack. I didn't mean for you and Dad to get hooked in."

"'Sokay."

Tony returned. "Hey man, they're gone and the lobby is almost clear. Let's get upstairs."

They moved as quickly as possible to the elevator and back to the room. By the time they arrived, his spasms had quit, replaced by the stiffness and aches they always left behind.

Sally stood and moved to his side. "Your back?"

Apparently she saw the answer in his face.

"Let's get you to bed."

"Don't know if I'm good for much action, babe."

She snorted. "You will be when I'm through with you."

Tony laughed, threw his arm around Cristal, and they left.

"Relax, I've got this," Sally told Carlos and Abby. "We have enough time to get Jack feeling better before leaving."

He grabbed her hand. "You're headed back to Blue Peak? I'd hoped—"

"Who said we're going home? You invited us to stay one more night and that's our plan." She helped him lie on the bed. "Besides, we wouldn't have room service, limousines, or mega-thread count sheets at home. This first class living you do is addictive."

Jack searched Sally's expression, identifying both a spark of humor and a wrinkle of worry.

"I've got some medication in the bathroom."

"You don't need Big Pharma when you've got me." She wiggled her fingers. "Prepare to find nirvana."

"Good band," he replied. He closed his eyes.

****

Sally closed the door to the bedroom and moved to the suite's seating area. She sank onto the chair across from Carlos and Abby.

Her son's forehead wrinkled. "How is he?"

"Sleeping. He'll be good to go by the time the car gets here."

"Mitch stopped by. He said to let Jack rest through sound check. He'll send a car later."

She let out a slow breath. "Good. Now all we have to do is keep Jack in bed."

Abby grinned. "I'm sure you'll find a way to handle that assignment."

Her face heated. "Resting. Jack needs a short bed rest."

"Right."

Abby drawled the word and gave it a twist. Sally avoided her stare by looking out the window.

"Mom, this back spasm thing. It's caused by stress, right?" Carlos's comment was more a statement than a question.

She studied her son's expression. "Could be." She shook her head. "You're the psychologist of the family. What's your diagnosis?"

"Yeah, that's what I thought." He laced his fingers with Abby's. "We've been talking, and we think the best thing is to grant an interview."

She opened and closed her mouth without voicing a thought.

"Yeah, I know that could create problems, but we figure combined with Cristal's statement, the interview may give us all a break. Besides, Jack's been the best father he could be under the circumstances, I hate to cause him pain."

Abby leaned forward. "I know you treasure your privacy and so do we. But the reporters won't leave until we give them something so bland, normal, they won't look for more."

Sally glanced between them. "You understand that your private wedding may be invaded. Reporters will try to crash your reception in case Jack is there. People you've known for years will treat you differently. All because of this news."

They exchanged glances. "We control who enters our home. We can hire security for the reception. We've already issued formal invitations to the reception, but it's not too late to mail out a card required for admittance."

"You've thought it out, I see. Have you also considered that one of your friends or customers could sell you out to the tabloids?"

"Then they'd be selling themselves out," Carlos said. "Because they'd be banned from the coffee house and the rest of my real friends would make sure they weren't welcome anywhere in town."

"Do you really think the folks in Blue Peak won't get behind us?" Abby asked. "I know I haven't lived there long, but that's one close-knit town."

"Abby's right, Mom. I'd like your approval on our plans because you're sure to get pulled in to the hoopla. But not responding to Dad's fame isn't healthy."

"My intuition insists this is a bad idea." She leaned back against the chair. "But, that could be my fear. You're right about not facing up to Jack's fans. I've never been one to deny the obvious."

Abby raised her eyebrows. "Excuse me? You've been denying your love for Jack for decades. When will you—"

Carlos placed his fingers over her mouth. "Shush. You know how stubborn she is."

When had her son taken a parental role? She didn't like the switch in positions. "Now see here, you two."

"Oh, I don't know. I wouldn't mind hearing more of what Abby has on her mind."

Jack's rough post-sleep voice sounded behind her. She looked over her shoulder at him leaning against the doorjamb with one hand behind his back. His jeans rode low on his hips, and he was shirtless. He scratched his broad chest, his fingers ruffling his salt and pepper hair. Her mouth watered.

"As I was saying," Abby began.

Sally held up her hand. "Hold it." She looked at Jack. "You should be in bed. Resting. The car isn't coming until later. Mitch is getting someone to fill in for sound check."

"Good." He pulled his hand from behind his back and waggled a small bottle. "The maid left a new bottle of bath oil. I thought you might like to try the stuff." He unscrewed the bottle and sniffed. "A little spicy. Like you."

Her face heated. "I don't think I want a bath, but thanks."

"Not so much fun when the sandal is on the other foot, is it, Sally?" Abby waggled her eyebrows.

She glared at her. "What do you mean?"

Her future daughter-in-law raised her eyebrows. "As I said. You think it's fine and dandy to push two people together, as long as you're not the one being persuaded."

"I didn't—"

"Don't even go there, Mom. She's got your number inked in gold leaf on parchment."

"Come on, babe. The spa jets will help with this pain I've got," Jack said.

His aura held a smidgen of darkness at the base of his spine. "Pain my ass."

He grinned. "Glad to know some things never change." He tilted the bottle in Sally's direction. "Hot water? Jets?"

She stood and pointed at Carlos. "Don't even think about copying your father's blatant attempts at seduction with Abby. She deserves suave."

Abby curled up against Carlos. "Oh, don't worry, Sally. He's got moves of his own."

She threw her hands over her ears. "Not what a mother wants to hear."

Carlos grinned. "No? Good. Then you'll stop bugging us about grandchildren."

Understanding she'd given away that bargaining point for now, she turned and headed for Jack. "Come on, big boy. Let's see about those jets."

****

She relaxed against Jack's chest. Hot, scented water lapped over the arms he'd wrapped around her.

"What about Abby and her mother? I don't want Abby losing her family over me," he said.

"You've met Marge. I called your mother. She's dealt with snobs for years. She can handle one more."

"My mother would like the opportunity to be a grandmother from more than at a distance."

His tone held a nuance she couldn't catch. Perhaps

he meant that Eleanor lived hundreds of miles away. Was she thinking of moving closer? What would that mean to all of them? Another thought dawned. She felt his chest rise in a long inhale, but interrupted before he could derail her sudden need for specific information.

"You never had more children, Jack. Why is that? I thought when you remarried you'd start a new family."

His muscles tensed under her. Her question had cued a rapid response.

"You mean because I acted as if I didn't have a family already?"

She caressed the back of his hands. "I apologize. I meant that Eleanor seems so happy to know Carlos, and your father—"

"Wanted a grandson to carry on the family name. Yeah."

His exhale felt cool against her wet hair.

"I had a vasectomy years ago. I wanted to stick it to my old man. You should have seen his face when I told him Carlos would be the only grandson he'd ever have."

She examined the light emanating from around his hands. "Your aura tells me something more, sweetie. That decision had more to do with conviction than emotional pain. What's the truth?"

"Crap. Now I know why Abby is learning this woo-woo shit from you. It's her only defense against your insights. Can men learn this crap?"

She pushed her elbow into his side.

"Oomph. Okay, I give."

His arms tightened around her.

"I couldn't stand losing you and Carlos. I never wanted to feel that pain again. Or make another person think I didn't care enough to be in their life." He rested his chin on her crown.

"Mitch told me. About your skating on the edge. I thought you enjoyed the parties. I believed—" she swallowed around a lump "—that you wanted the high life more than us."

He rested his cheek against hers. "Shh. Not important."

"Jack, how can the very public life you lead not be important? I've seen the way everyone caters to you, gives you stuff even before you ask. Criminy, this life is addictive. I'd maim someone to have a bathroom like this. And the fluffy towels? Pure heaven."

"I meant the past, babe. We'll figure out the future as we go, okay?"

"Okay, yes. You're right."

He kissed the back of her neck. "Would a dozen do?"

"A dozen of what?"

"The towels. I'll have the concierge send a dozen to you. Unless you want more in some other colors?"

Her laughter echoed off the marble even as she wondered what he held back.

## Chapter Twenty

"Dad, I asked Mitch to arrange an interview with a reporter from the same station Cristal called." Carlos looked worried but not afraid. "We thought it'd be good to have both stories air on the same day. Get the hassle over with. They'll be here in a few minutes."

"I wish you'd have checked with me first." Jack clenched his jaw. "You don't need to expose yourself this way, Carlos. Not to mention giving me a little advance notice."

"I didn't want to interrupt your bath," Carlos said.

Jack slammed a fist to his hip. "I don't need your protection, but you sure as hell need mine. I'm sitting in and you can bet your ass I'll shut the reporter down at the first sign of trouble."

"And I'm the one who pushed Jack from your life, so I'll be here, too," Sally said.

"Babe, you don't know what you're saying. This won't be a college symposium. The scene could get nasty, quick. Don't open your life up for me."

"That's enough from both of you," Carlos said. "I'm an adult. I can handle this. Besides, we won't be talking with a Sunday night national news reporter known for hard-hitting interviews. Mitch promised. He said he knew who to ask. A woman who is thorough but fair, someone who owes him a favor."

Jack ran his hands through his hair. "Christ. This

doesn't feel right."

"Now you sound like Mom," Carlos said.

"Is that such a bad thing?"

"Nope." The two shared grins.

A knock sounded at the door. Jack checked his watch. "That's gotta be Mitch with the reporter. Are we ready?" He caught Sally's eye. "Last chance."

"Don't worry. I won't blame you if something goes wrong."

A chill hit his spine. He hoped she wouldn't change her mind later, after he told her about the P.I. reports. He opened the door and his gut churned. Not a woman reporter, but the dickhead who'd gotten Cristal on tape that morning. This guy was a cluster waiting to happen.

Mitch bustled in and pulled Jack aside. "I know, man. Not what we expected. My reporter choice had a family emergency."

Jack groaned.

"Look, if we cancel now, it'll look bad. Carlos committed to an interview with the station, not a specific person. If they want to switch representatives, they have that right." He placed his hand on Jack's shoulder. "I'm sitting in on this. Don't worry."

He wanted to rail at Mitch. Instead, he watched the reporter and cameraman check out the suite. He figured they conferred on the best camera angles while speculating on sleeping arrangements. "Mitch, I want your promise that you'll shut them down the second it looks like the interview is going south. Got that?"

"Goes without saying."

Mitch could be trusted in a tight spot. That hadn't and wouldn't change. Too bad Jack couldn't trust himself. He'd walked away from his family instead of learning how to protect them. Time to grow some balls.

The reporter held out his hand. "Sig Daniels. We didn't have a chance to introduce ourselves last time we met."

Jack eyed his hand then grasped it and shook. He introduced his family and settled next to Sally on the couch. Carlos and Abby were on the love seat across from them. Mitch stood next to the cameraman.

"I understand you want to talk about the recent statement regarding your father," Sig said to Carlos. "Would you mind giving me some background, first?"

Jack loosened his involuntary fists when he noticed the camera pointing his way.

"Actually, I'd like to stick to my prepared statement." His son's tone was cool, yet polite. He handed a page to Sig. "I've made a copy for you."

"But you'll be giving me a chance to get more details, right?"

A smile flitted across Carlos's face. "If you have questions about the statement, sure."

His muscles loosened. Carlos acted as if he handled interviews every day. Not that he'd relax his guard. He'd been trapped one too many times over the years, and Sig Daniels reminded him of every chop-busting reporter he'd ever met.

Unease grew as Daniels lobbed softball questions to Carlos. He'd seen this soften-the-subject-then-whap-them approach before. His back muscles tightened. Sally glanced at him then winked. Didn't help, but he appreciated her gesture.

"So, Carlos, you seem pretty comfortable with your father. I'm surprised. I think most of the viewers watching would be more than a little angry. Not only did you miss out on the opportunities a rich father could have given you, he didn't show for your activities. He didn't attend your cum laude graduation." He leaned forward. "He never contacted you, not once. That's gotta tick you off, man. Unless he bought you off before this interview."

He felt more than heard Sally's gasp.

"I'm convinced my parents took the actions they thought best for me. Besides, my dad kept up with my progress. That told me he never stopped caring."

Her body stiffened next to his.

"Really? Kept up with you in what ways?"

Carlos clenched his fists. Uh-oh. Getting angry with Daniels was not a good sign. *You've done great, son, don't blow it now.*

Carlos glanced at his parents, but Jack couldn't read his expression.

"Not part of our joint statement, but I agreed to this interview to set the record straight. You spoke with Cristal and know that Jack isn't her father. Jack kept quiet to protect her and her real father. He used the same discretion with me. I know he got regular reports on me, I've seen the photos. That's why I'm not angry."

"But what about his not bothering—"

Carlos made a slashing motion with his hand. "No more on this topic. Do you have other questions? If not, we're done here."

Daniels kept his gaze on Carlos, and whatever he saw there must have convinced him the interview had ended. He motioned to his cameraman and shook hands with Carlos before leaving.

The room door had barely shut behind the

television people and Mitch before Sally turned on him.

"Regular reports, Jack? What the hell does that mean?"

*Busted.*

Carlos moved to her side and hugged her shoulders. "Cool it, Mom. Nana Young showed me photos. Dad didn't explain yet?"

"Explain what, exactly?"

Jack tightened his grip on Sally. "I started to tell you, but the timing never seemed right or we were interrupted. Besides, my past actions were more about Carlos than you."

"He's right, Mom," Carlos said. "Nana told me she needed to know I was safe. She couldn't come visit us. Even if Grandfather had let her travel, you wouldn't have allowed her in the house."

Sally moved to the side and crossed her arms. "You still haven't explained your actions, Jack. What reports? What photos? And how long has this been going on?"

"Come on, Mom, you know we were interrupted earlier. Still, I thought he'd have told you at least the basics by now."

"He hasn't said a word, and I know we've had time to talk." Her glare made his balls shrink. "I think you'd better leave and let us discuss this."

Abby grabbed Carlos's arm and they sprinted for the door, stopping only to snag a room key.

\*\*\*\*

Sally turned on her heel to face Jack. "You, or was it your mother hired someone to follow Carlos? Did I infer correctly?"

He nodded slowly, as if looking for a trap. "My

mother did, against my father's express wishes. It was the first time she ever went up against him, even secretly."

She tapped her foot. "How often? Daily, weekly, monthly, what?"

"The reports? Monthly, at first."

"For how long? How long did she snoop?"

"Only until he cleared grade school."

"Baloney, Jack. Carlos made it sound like the reports never stopped. Is that true?"

He cleared his throat. "Well, I took over the contract, but the report frequency went to quarterly once I knew—"

"Once you figured I wouldn't abandon him? Or what, take him off to live in a dirty commune? Or an ashram?"

His face reddened. His hands clenched. "No. Once I knew he'd make it through high school without going off the deep end. Then the reports went to yearly."

"How could you have someone spy on us?"

"Do you really think I'd walk away from my son? My only child?"

She should have known he wouldn't, but that wasn't a fact she'd admit to now. "So all this talk about trust is baloney. You've never trusted me. Not really. Would you have violated the divorce agreement? Sure, of course you would have. You waited for me to screw up, didn't you?"

"True, I didn't trust you then. Can you blame me? We've talked about what happened. Hell, I thought we were past that."

Her chest hurt. She felt lightheaded and forced air into her lungs.

"This big reunion, pretending you didn't know how Carlos and I lived, that was for show. All along you had some, some *snoop* digging through our lives. Low, Jack, really low."

"Fine, blame this on me. I stuck to our agreement, Sally, long past the time Carlos turned eighteen." He put his fist on his hip. "And you know what? He wasn't anywhere near as upset about the investigator as you are. He gets it. He gets that I needed some way to stay in touch. What is so fucking wrong with that?"

"Sounds like stalking to me."

"Bullshit. I had someone deliver regular reports. I didn't sit outside your house with binoculars. Big difference."

"Well, how would you like someone watching your every move when you thought you were living a private life?" She executed a face palm and held up her other hand. "Never mind." She inhaled through her nose. "Obviously you're accustomed to rock star notoriety."

"Don't. Don't use my past actions as an excuse to fight with me now. And you know I think fame can suck like a black hole. What's really going on here, Sally?"

She hugged herself. "Us. Getting back together. It won't work."

"Why not?"

His quiet tone didn't fool her. He was about thirty seconds from exploding. "I don't fit in this life, Jack, and I never will."

"This is my last tour. I promise. I've already told the guys I'm not going out again. Besides, earlier you said you could get used to the high life. You joked about maiming to get a fancy bathroom, for crap's sake."

She raised her eyebrows.

"Okay, so that wasn't the best choice of words. But I want to give you so much, and you throw everything I am back in my face every chance you get. I'm a human being. A guy who loves you. Who walked away, yeah, but who knows better now. Tell me, exactly, why two people who know what life is like without a soul deep love can't work out a few problems? Give me the fucking time of day, why don't you."

She took a deep breath and fought for calm. "Privacy, Jack. It's not fun to have your life ripped to shreds without warning."

"You mean like mine when Carlos called out of the blue? After the shock, I embraced the change. That's what you tell people to do, isn't it? In your shop?"

She pursed her lips. Damn him for being right.

"What happened to the Sally I knew? That Sally was up for adventure, taking charge. She didn't hide out in fear. Because that whole privacy thing, that's what I see, an excuse to put up another wall."

"People with money think they can do anything. Invading my privacy is not something I can easily accept," she countered. "No, I don't see keeping my business to myself as putting up freaking walls." At some level, she knew she lied, but that issue could keep until she had, yes, time alone.

She held up her hand when he opened his mouth. "And don't say your investigator only followed Carlos. I was in charge of his life, so obviously he reported on me, also." Jack didn't speak, giving her a default answer.

"I think we've pretty much said enough. I can't be

with you. Please leave me alone while I pack." She turned on her heel and entered the bedroom. Once the door was shut, she leaned against it and hugged herself.

She'd known she could never be enough for Jack. Getting back with her ex had always been an idea too good to be true.

Chapter Twenty-One

Sally's jaw dropped. She sat in her car one hundred feet from her store. A large group comprised mostly of men, some with cameras, others with microphones, hung around outside Good Vibes. She doubted they waited for the latest shipment of Nag Champa incense.

She settled herself with a few deep breaths, repressed the urge to drive home, and stepped from the car. She had a business to run.

As she approached, several reporters glanced in her direction, then away. She assumed that they hadn't yet recognized her with her hair down and wearing normal clothes. Well, normal for her. It wasn't until she moved to the door, key in hand, that questions came simultaneously.

"Are you Mrs. Jack Reed?"

"Why'd you keep your marriage secret?"

"Do you have any other children you're hiding? Are they from another rock star?"

"Did you divorce Jack before he got famous or did he ditch you after the band hit?"

"How long has your son owned the coffee house across the street?"

"Did Jack buy the business for him?"

"How much money did Jack pay in child support?"

"Why did he hide you and your son? Is there mental illness in the family?"

"Are you in a threesome with Jack and Glynnis?"

Many other questions had been called out that she hadn't heard, hadn't wanted to acknowledge. The lock tumbled, but she didn't open her door or enter. Instead, she braced herself against the glass and wood, turning to face the group.

"For the record, my name is Sally Ford, not Mrs. Jack Reed. My marriage to Jack was a long time ago and had nothing to do with his rock career. I think the reason neither of us spoke about our marriage to the press is obvious right now, don't you? I really don't have anything to add to the statement that has already been issued."

She turned to enter. One loud question boomed above the rest. "Are you a witch?"

Her hand stilled on the knob. The set of her shoulders, or perhaps her stillness, alerted the group that the inquiry had struck a nerve. They grew quiet. Waited for dirt.

Swiveling, she looked at the crowd. "Who asked that question?"

Sig Daniels raised his hand.

"I should have known."

He smirked.

"Well, Mr. Daniels, let me educate you. Polytheistic practices are ancient and—"

"I can get that information from Wikipedia. My question was, are *you* a witch?"

"Right now, I wish I could cast a spell turning you into a mute frog, but unfortunately, I can't do that." The reporters laughed. "Pagan practitioners use their energy for good."

"Nice reply *Ms.* Ford, but you didn't answer the

question. Are you or aren't you a witch?" He waved toward the store window, which featured a display on harvesting herbs and native plants for healing. "Sure looks like it to me."

"Do you need glasses, *Mr.* Daniels? Herbology is not witchcraft."

Another reporter called out. "Yeah, but you still haven't answered, lady."

"You did it for me. If I'm a lady, I'm not a witch, right?" She pushed open the door behind her. "Now, I have a business to run. As I said earlier, I'm not adding to the published statement. You all are welcome to come in and browse." She pointed to the card posted on her door that had been hidden by her body. "Long-standing store policy. You don't need shoes or shirts for service, but no photographs allowed."

A patrol car slowed to a stop in front of Good Vibes. She waved to the policeman. "Hey, Joe."

"Morning, Sally. You need any help?"

"No, just a group of excited customers waiting to empty my store of self-help books."

"I'll be close by, Sally." He cast a dark look over the group. "Call if you need me to throw out any trespassers or other trouble makers."

"Will do, Joe. Thanks."

He nodded and put his car in gear, moving off at less than five miles per hour.

"Now, gentlemen and ladies, Good Vibes is open for the day." She paused. "Of course, I know you have more important things to do, like filing stories and following leads. Don't let me stop you. There's nothing in my store that you can't find elsewhere." She located Daniels and caught his gaze. "Including books on herbs and natural healing."

At that, she entered and stashed her purse below the counter. Several of the group, including Sig Daniels, followed her and nosed around. The others headed across the street to Carlos's coffee house. Her hands shook. She hadn't expected reporters outside her door this early. She eyed the store. Certainly not inside her business.

She could kill Jack if she didn't miss him like crazy.

****

Carlos walked in to Good Vibes whistling what sounded like the old standard, "Witchcraft."

"Very funny," Sally said.

"You're a witch, I'm a wizard. The news reports said so."

"A wizard with coffee drinks is a far cry from an older woman being called a witch."

He pulled her into a hug. "You may have more years than me—"

"That's a given."

"But, you're not old."

"Good save." She moved behind her counter. "So, are you ready for your wedding? Nervous? Want to elope, instead?"

He leveled his finger at her. "Not getting out of your commitment that easily, Mom."

She shrugged. "Worth a try."

"Do you really hate Dad that much?"

"Oh, sweetie, I don't hate Jack, only his lifestyle."

"But he's not going to tour anymore. You could see the world with him. He's a great travel companion. Or expand the store. He wouldn't care as long as you're together."

"What are you, his ambassador of goodwill?"

He narrowed his eyes. "What are you, jealous?"

She sighed. "My son, the Doctor of Psychology."

Carlos wiggled his fingers in a "gimme me" gesture.

"Yes, I'm jealous. Jealous, angry, hurt, confused, and, in love with your father." The last slipped off her tongue without conscious thought. Not that it was anything Carlos hadn't already determined for himself. "And frustrated with the reporters for taking photos against my wishes."

"So what. They take bad photos on purpose. Dad comes off tour on Sunday. You should see his last concert in Washington. He'd send a plane ticket. Hell, he'd send a private jet. What's stopping you?"

"Are you kidding? You, the recipient of focused media attention? The latest network wonder? You know how I feel about privacy, and you're wondering why I'm not with Jack?" She huffed. "And 'last concert?' " Really? You believe he's giving up music?"

"He's giving up touring, not music. He'll be making music when I'm a grandfather, I hope. In fact, he told me last night he's working on a new solo project. Acoustic songs for meditation, or massage, or something quiet. Can't tour with those."

"He's…what did you say?"

"You heard me. Go to his last concert, Mom. He wants you there."

"What about you and Abby?"

"We wouldn't miss it." He put his hands on her shoulders. "He started his touring career with you, and he wants you in at the end. So put your pride in your back pocket, or better yet, release it to the ethers the way you advise others and agree."

She wavered. Could she see Jack again without jumping his bones? She'd have to, because she'd told him they were over.

Too bad her love didn't know how to say good-bye.

\*\*\*\*

"She said yes?" Jack breathed for the first time since answering the call from Carlos. "Great, I mean, good, that's good."

"Only good? You're so full of shit, your eyes are brown, Dad."

"Oh, so genes have nothing to do with it? Glad you told me."

They discussed the trip and the wedding. Jack hung up. Everything was on track. His plan had to work. He called Mitch to ensure everything was under control.

"Are you serious about this Jack?"

"As the opening horn riff of 'Sledgehammer.' "

"Your family knows what they're in for, right? No running off in a huff after I send the plane?"

He swallowed his doubt. "They know."

"Fine. I've already got Kathy working out a travel plan."

"Thanks. Do you also have the press release ready to send out after the last show?"

"One more time, Jack. Are you sure?"

"Sledgehammer." He rubbed his chest. The words felt like a sledgehammer to his heart.

His manager sighed. "Yeah. I'll hand out a copy to the band later this afternoon. You know the drill by now."

"Sure, all copies come back to you for security. Relax, Mitch. The news should give Grant's son's band another kick up the ladder. They're gonna be big."

"I know."

"Shit, Mitch. You may as well say, 'I told you so.' Or are you waiting to hear me admit getting us out on this tour was the right thing to do?"

"Whatever you want to admit to, man."

"Ball buster. Fine. You were right. But so am I about no more tours."

"I hear ya."

After the call ended, Jack reached for his guitar to work out a new riff. He thought about calling his first solo album, "Bewitched."

His thoughts spun out as his fingers moved over the strings.

He'd need to do more than bewitch Sally back. No spells or links forged of lust. This time he meant to keep her. For good.

\*\*\*\*

Sally, Carlos, and Abby left the private jet at Dulles in the late afternoon. When they walked from the secure area to the public concourse, a uniformed driver stood with a sign reading "Ford."

"Dad delivered," Carlos said.

She felt her stomach flip. One step closer to Jack.

They rode in silence, going directly to the auditorium. The chauffeur must have alerted Mitch to their arrival time because he waited for them.

He nodded. "Sally."

She was surprised he spoke to her given her precipitate escape from the Charlotte hotel. Jack must not have told Mitch that she'd called it quits.

He escorted them through check-in to Jack's dressing room, which stood empty. "Jack is with the band, but he'd like you to wait for him here. He'll be back in a few."

Carlos sank into the couch and checked his tablet. Abby nestled against his shoulder and closed her eyes. That left her with little to do but worry.

Had Jack really wanted her here in Washington, or was this her son's attempt to push them together? She wouldn't put it past Abby to stick in her two cents, either. Damn. She never should have agreed to make the trip.

Jack pushed open the door. "Hey, guys. Glad you're here."

He didn't avoid her, but neither was his greeting hug overlong or too tight. Damn. She should have insisted on staying home.

"Want a bite to eat? The caterer Mitch hired knocked herself out with the food."

She checked his aura and didn't see anything out of the ordinary. She stood and moved toward the door. "I'm hungry. Come on, you two. You told me you haven't eaten much today."

Carlos waved his hand in a shooing motion. "Go ahead, Mom. I have to finish this e-mail to a vendor."

Abby yawned. "Yeah, go ahead. I'll stay with Carlos."

She knew without checking auras that they were up to mischief. "Not a problem. I can wait and go in with you."

Jack snorted. "Are you auditioning for a birth control gig? I think they want a few minutes alone."

Abby put her hand over her mouth, her shoulders

shaking.

"Oh, sure, fine. I'll, um, okay, I'll go on without you." She would tell the kids what she thought of their matchmaking plans later.

She followed Jack out the door. When he moved closer, she backed herself into a corner. He put one arm on the wall above her head.

"I was hoping you'd wear that hot black number you had on in Charlotte." His gaze raked her from head to toe. "But what you've got on works."

She smoothed her hands down her skirt. Tonight she wore a purple velvet wrap skirt with a turquoise silk top and a multi-colored scarf that incorporated both colors. She'd pulled her hair up and used hair ornaments. Nothing about her outfit was overtly sexy, but Jack's regard made her feel like Salome waiting to dance.

Sally looked him over. He looked particularly yummy dressed all in black. His pants clung to muscular thighs and tight ass. The shirt he wore emphasized his shoulders and played up his brown eyes. She could eat him up with a spoon. A tiny baby food spoon so the treat would last longer.

He licked his lips. His pupils darkened. "Glad you came tonight."

"Thanks for sending the plane, but it wasn't necessary. We could have flown commercial." She inhaled. "But it was fun. I've never been on a private jet. Do you travel that way all the time?"

"Nah. We use a tricked out bus for shorter tours like this one. I enjoyed sending the plane, you know that, right?" His voice lowered. "I wanted to make sure you showed." He ran his fingers through his hair.

"These last tour dates have been hell."

His scent surrounded her, confusing her thoughts. She finally managed a response. "Yeah, the media exposure has been brutal toward you."

"Media? Shit, no. I've...never mind." He ran a calloused fingertip over her cheekbone. "I'm sorry you had to handle the news people alone. I never meant for that to happen."

She pushed her shoulders back. "It was my decision to leave, remember?"

His finger pressed against her lips. "Shh. Enough about my screw ups. Tonight is about the future." He glanced over his shoulder at the bustle of the Rough Cuts crew. "Besides this isn't the best place to talk. Let's get something to eat and drink."

He threw his arm over her shoulders and directed her to another room down the corridor.

They joined the rest of the band and their families. Sally filled a small plate with food but couldn't choke any down. Jack's heat surrounded her and once again, she found herself drawn into his orbit. Luckily, Carlos and Abby joined her along with Tony's wife, Liz.

Liz clinked her glass against Sally's. "To the tour's end."

"I'll drink to that." A glass of wine later, she could breathe freely again, though that might have had more to do with Jack standing across the room than having totally relaxed.

She and Liz stood together, watching the group's camaraderie. Once again, Sally was struck by the easy energy flow between people. Jack had a family, a big one. Many of the people here tonight had been tight with him since the start. She understood Jack's need to

239

know Carlos, but where did she fit in? Did he, could he still love her after she'd blown him off? She couldn't deny her feelings for her ex, but with Jack keeping his distance, she thought possibly she'd blown her final chance with him. Probably.

"You know," Liz began, "Tony and I live at the beach for part of the year."

"I wasn't aware." Was she going somewhere with this?

"Walking the beach keeps me sane when Tony's writing. You have no idea how hearing the same limited number of chords repeated for three hours can drive me bananas." She grinned. "So over the years, I've collected multiple jars of sea glass."

"Lucky you. I haven't been to the beach since I opened my store. I don't often take vacations, though I do shorten my hours when school is out."

"That's too bad. I'd hoped you'd come to visit."

"I'd like that," Sally said.

"I'll show you my favorite places to find sea glass." Liz shifted closer. "The thing I like about sea glass is that garbage gets dumped into the ocean, but the water takes the pollution, polishes jagged edges smooth, and adds texture to man's carelessness. And when the glass is returned, it's beautiful. I never tire of the metaphor."

"You mean when life's sharp edges cut us, we can choose to smooth the path we face?"

Liz smiled. "That's one way to look at it."

"May I ask you a personal question?"

Liz nodded.

"Did you feel comfortable with Glynnis coming to see Cristal and the band over the years? She's the kind of woman who, well I wouldn't trust her. And what she did to Billy was cold."

"Glynnis is a mess, no doubt about that." Liz tilted her head. "But you know, we figured she wasn't the one pouring booze down Billy's throat. And Cristal is a gift. Things equal out over lifetimes, right?"

Her words struck a chord with Sally. She'd said basically the same thing to Jack. So why had she allowed her back to get up over Glynnis? The woman needed compassion, not anger.

"Yes, you're right," Sally said. "I feel like a fool for ignoring the basic principles of karma. Thanks for reminding me."

Liz looked over Sally's shoulder, smiled, and slipped off.

Sally felt Jack's heat along her spine. He whispered in her ear.

"I've missed you, babe. Like one of my arms. Or my picking fingers."

"I've missed you too." She took a deep breath. "I thought about that. That I screwed up. Again." She turned to face him. "Our timing sucks, doesn't it?"

"The band's big announcement about touring breaks tomorrow morning."

She put her hand on his arm. "Jack, don't you think you should wait until the Carlos story dies down?"

He shook his head. "No. Get the word out now and both stories will blow over faster."

"I hope no one blames Carlos for your decision to stop touring."

He put his fingers over her lips. "Reporters are in the room."

She froze. "Damnation."

"That's why I've been making the rounds, to divert attention from you guys. After the show, you, Carlos, and Abby have me all to yourselves." He waggled his eyebrows. "I hope you know what to do with me."

A slow grin reached her lips. "I'll think of something while you're busy on stage."

Mitch put his fingers between his lips and gave a shrill whistle. The Rough Cuts members began moving toward the door.

"Gotta run, babe. Can't wait for later." He kissed her cheek and sauntered off.

Chapter Twenty-Two

Sally, Carlos, and Abby joined other family members in the wings. Since adding "Eyes of Love" to their Charlotte show, the band had pulled out other old songs they hadn't recently performed for succeeding dates, rehearsing each during sound checks and days off. The last set they'd play tonight would feature those tunes. Their set changes had sparked media questions. Fans grabbed the opportunity to turn each concert into a guessing game. Which "new" old song would the Cuts play that night?

Everyone's questions would be answered the following morning. The knowledge made her jittery. She hoped Jack wouldn't take heat for the decision, even though the band wives were happy their husbands were slowing down. They all knew that none of the guys would retire—the word wasn't in their vocabulary. The Rough Cuts were and always had been a workhorse band. She fully expected Jack to go back out on the road within three years. That's the way the band rolled. Plus, they had a fortieth anniversary as a band to celebrate, soon.

She didn't know if she and Jack would be together at that point. Or even after tonight. She'd thought her life had been lived with courage, but he'd shown her the fear that had ruled her heart. A legacy of regret would be hers unless she took a leap of faith and trusted

Jack. One more night together would be better than never feeling him inside her again.

Carlos pulled her into a two-step dance and bent to speak into her ear. "What's wrong?"

"Wrong?" His question put her thoughts into sudden perspective. "Nothing, sweetie. Not now." She smiled at him and swung him in Abby's direction. Her choice? No more fear. Going after her wish wasn't such a hard decision, after all.

Heart at ease she danced, throwing in a shimmy or two after catching Jack's eye. She didn't care who watched, that man would be hers.

When the last set rocked to a close, the band ran into the wings accompanied by the sound of roof-raising cheers and stomping feet. Jack's chest heaved as he snagged a towel and water bottle.

"The last encore will be for you, babe."

Tears welled. "Sweetie, I want you to know, I've changed my mind about sticking. If it's not too late."

Apprehension flashed across his face. He raised his eyebrows. "Not too late?"

"No matter what happens tomorrow, or even in thirty minutes, you top my hit parade. You always will."

He pulled her against him, thrust his fingers into her hair, and planted his lips over hers. She heard Carlos whooping behind them.

Jack lifted his head and stepped back. "Damn, babe. I'm all sweaty. I think I ruined your blouse."

He was right. Her silk blouse was damp in spots corresponding to his chest height. She grinned. "I'm thinking it'll make a good souvenir of your last concert. If I go broke, I can sell the blouse on E-Bay. Will you autograph and date it for me?"

"Nope." He lifted her chin. "This blouse is a keepsake for our grandkids."

Tony slapped Jack on the back and spoke over his shoulder as he moved past. "Let's go, man. Time to wrap this up."

Jack gave her a quick kiss. "For luck, babe."

She watched them move back onstage, her heart in her throat. Could be she hadn't blown her chance after all.

\*\*\*\*

The Rough Cuts had ended the night playing their first big hit, "Eyes of Love." Now champagne flowed in the Green Room.

Jack rested his elbow on Tony's shoulder and sipped bubbly, though he'd prefer beer. Normally, everyone scattered for home as soon as the last encore faded. Tonight, their crew stuck together, discussing the evening's highlights. He appreciated the private time. Even though they'd stay in touch, always in closer contact than many families, the scene held poignancy they wouldn't admit feeling.

His eyes narrowed. Someone had admitted two reporters, who chose the opportunity of finding the band together to interrupt. One of the men, tall and thin with greased-back hair and heavy black-rimmed glasses tapped Jack on the shoulder.

"Jack, we've just heard that tonight was your last concert. Care to make a statement?"

"Not really. We're having a private minute, here." He scanned the room. "Mitch is in the corner." He pointed. "Talk to him."

"Are you having a private moment because this

was your last concert? Are you all quitting the music industry?"

Already keyed up, Jack's hands fisted. "I don't think you heard me. I'm not talking, but Mitch is." He turned his back on the reporter.

Who didn't take the hint. "We've heard your first ex-wife has asked you to stop touring. Is that right? Are you getting back with her?"

"You've got your facts wrong, and this is your business, why?" Jack exhaled through his nose. "Look, you're blowing my high. If you don't get lost, I'll ask Security to lose you for me."

"So the rumor is true? You're quitting music at the request of your secret family? You feeling guilty for leaving them behind all those years ago?"

Jack made a sudden move, but Tony had a hand on his shoulder before he could deliver the physical reply he wanted to give. He settled for a glare. "Get. Lost." He narrowed his eyes. "Got it?"

The reporters backed off looking nervous. "Yeah, got it." They located Mitch and headed in his direction.

"You know you gave him a story," Tony said.

"Fuck me, yeah." He checked Sally's location and saw she was standing with Liz and Abby. He knew he'd have to tell her what happened. Disheartened, he turned back to his buddies. "We had a hell of a show tonight."

"We had a hell of a tour," Dougie, the bassist, said.

The men nodded and smiled at each other.

"I'd say let's do it again next year," Jack said, "but you know I'd be lying."

They laughed and made plans to gather over the holidays. Jack joined Sally, who was now flanked by Carlos and Abby. He put his arm around her. "Ready to go?"

"You betcha," she said. She went up on tiptoe and whispered in his ear. "I've figured out what I want to do with you."

When he was younger, those words, in that voice, would have given him an instant boner. As it was, he had a respectable start. He steered them toward the door and into a flash of cameras. He held up his hand. "Tour is over, guys. Give us a break, hey?"

Sally placed her hand in the middle of his back, and her touch helped him recover the calm that had slipped. He drew her under his arm.

"I'm beat. Want to kick back at the hotel." He flashed his trademark grin. "Us old farts need our sleep. Can't play those two hour plus shows and party all night anymore."

A young man clad in mostly black leather said, "We'll be quick, Jack. We're wondering why you played nothing but old songs in your second set tonight, in a departure from every previous tour. Social media posts are running wild."

"Other people's speculation is not my problem," he answered.

A short, scruffy man called out next. "Yeah, and you didn't start playing old hits until the Charlotte date, halfway through your schedule. Word is you're giving up music and settling in the sticks."

"Told you, man, I just want to lay out at the hotel. Sooner than later."

A woman's voice chimed. "Did your first wife put a spell on you, Jack? That's her next to you, right? I heard she sells voodoo dolls in that witchcraft store she owns."

"If she can get someone like Jack, I'll buy a dozen kits," a second woman yelled.

Sally's muscles tightened under his hand. Before he could take a breath to reply, her voice sounded over the melee.

"Now, hush. Shame on all y'all. Jack and the rest of the band shared their souls with you tonight. They played their hearts out, and you stand out here wanting another piece of him. He's being polite and answering your questions when any fool with half a brain can see he's exhausted. Oh, wait. I forgot my audience. Now, shoo. It's past time we were away." She waved her hand as if conducting an orchestra. "Clear us a path, why don't you. Thank you, kindly."

Two of the reporters drew back, and Sally pushed him in their direction as security guards arrived to help escort them out.

He bent to her ear level, ignoring the cameras flashing behind them. "Thank you, kindly? What were you doing? Channeling a Southern belle?"

"I can put on the Scarlett when required," she said.

I've never called you Red because you told me you'd feed me my balls if I did, but I'm reconsidering whether I need my testicles now that I've seen your Scarlettness."

She arched a brow. "Scarlettness? You don't want to go there. Besides, I like your testicles right where they are. For now." She winked.

The partial hard-on that had faded when they ran into the reporters returned with a vengeance. Damn. How'd he ever lived without her? Would she still be willing to join her life with his now that reporters dogged their steps?

\*\*\*\*

In the hotel suite, they grabbed drinks from the mini-bar and chatted together until Carlos and Abby retired.

Jack grabbed a battered guitar she recognized as the one he used when they were married. "I've got a new song I want to play for you. I'd like your opinion."

The intro caught her heart along with her attention. He segued into another rhythm and began singing about old love that stood the test of time. About a couple growing old together. Her heart stuttered.

He ended the song, turned, and took her hands in his. She knew his inhalation had pulled all the air from the room because her lungs couldn't find oxygen. Calloused finger pads moved across the backs of her hands, causing a shiver along her spine.

"I had a speech prepared, but all I can say is, I love you. I've loved you since I first saw you in that long, flowing dress, standing in the mud at Woodstock. Sally, I was too stupid to know what I, we, had, but I do know we can have something better. Will you believe my life isn't all rude reporters and invasive news stories? I don't want that night in Charlotte to be the last time we make love together."

Her brain stopped working.

"Sally? It's never too late to love. Anything is possible, at any age. Just, you know, I'd like to take that chance sooner than later."

"I—" *I don't know what to say.*

His palm lightly cupped her chin. "Are you in there?"

"Ahh—" *Holy Goddess. This could be my last chance.*

"Now you're scaring me."

She felt his hand on her shoulder and a slight shaking motion. His head tipped toward hers. "Sally? Babe? Are you okay?"

He looked blurry. No wonder. Her eyes were wet.

He pulled her against his side, his cheek resting on her head. "I'm such a dumb shit. I guess I shouldn't have sprung this on you, but I've waited so damn long for you already. I don't want to waste any more time away. Ever."

Jack had waited for her. Isn't that what she'd been doing? Waiting? Waiting for her life to begin, for another special man to come along, for romance, companionship, love? His heart beat strong and fast under her ear. She'd been wrong about protecting her privacy above all else. Love took courage and opening yourself to the world.

She looked up and put her hand on his jaw. "Oh, Jack. I do love you, you know that right?" She cleared her throat to rid her voice of the rusty gate sound. "I must be crazy." Her head felt like an explosion loomed.

He leaned forward, wrapped his hands around the back of her neck and moved his mouth over hers in a gentle and long kiss.

When he released her she had trouble focusing her eyes. He kept surprising her. She wasn't ready for this, not yet. But could she walk away again?

\*\*\*\*

Jack ran his fingers through this hair. *Well, her non-answer sucked, unless he counted the kiss as her answer. If so, there was hope.*

"Yes," Sally said.

"What?" He caught his breath. Had he heard

correctly?

She lightly squeezed his hands. "I not only still love you Jack, I trust you. I trust you with my life. I believe you will always work to protect me. Carlos and Abby, too." She leaned her head on his shoulder. "I'm tired of fighting, sweetie. Fighting myself as much as you."

His heart flipped. He wanted to stab his fist in the air, but settled for wrapping his arms around her.

"You got me." Tears streamed down her face. "Those damn pictures you kept grabbed my heart, but then you wrote a song that tore it right from my chest, I swannee."

His heart felt too big for his chest. He cupped her cheeks with his palms and swooped in for a kiss. "Babe, I can't wait to take you anywhere you want to go. Stonehenge, the Great Pyramids, Machu Picchu, you name it."

Her stomach growled. "How about to the restaurant for a late dinner? I was too nervous to eat earlier."

"I'll call down to room service." He laid an open-mouthed kiss to the hollow of her throat. "I'm all for having dessert while we wait for them."

"I'm up for that."

He inhaled her spicy scent and brushed his lips over her temple. "Yeah, do you know what you want me to order?"

"I've changed my mind about room service. All I want is you."

Chapter Twenty-Three

"Do you, Carlos Jonathan Young, take this woman Abigail Grace Stephens, to be your lawfully wedded wife?"

Sally watched the scene, her heart full to bursting. Late afternoon sunshine entered the windows, throwing a glow around Carlos and Abby. Henry and Bunny sat calmly at their owner's feet, wedding rings on ribbons loosely tied around their necks. They'd walked in, planted themselves, and hadn't moved since the ceremony began. She had no doubt they understood their role in the wedding.

Her gaze tangled with Jack's. He didn't try to hide his damp eyes from her. With a few more words, their son would be married to the love of his life. She'd lost her belief in happily ever after, but had regained it when Jack returned.

What was marriage between two loving people but the triumph of hope and trust? She glanced at Jack. They'd had plenty of hope but no trust when they'd married. She knew now that while the hurt she'd felt when they split had been all too real, Eleanor had been right. They hadn't been ready for each other then. They may not make it now, even given life's lessons. But if they didn't succeed as a couple, it wouldn't be because they had no trust or hope.

And that realization was the biggest gift she'd ever

given herself or Jack.

Her gaze took in Carlos and Abby's first kiss as a married couple. Even if she hadn't been able to read their auras, she'd have thought they glowed. Her throat tightened. She knew Jack planned to perform the song he'd played for her after his last concert in Washington. She hoped she didn't start bawling when he sang.

She noticed Margaret kept a healthy distance from her ex-husband and his new wife. She knew all about the anger and fear that kept people apart. Maybe, if Margaret were encouraged, she'd dismount her high horse and actually talk to her former spouse. If Sally had enough to drink, she may recommend the action.

After everyone congratulated the newly wedded couple, she moved to Jack's side. He picked up his guitar and perched at the end of a chair in front of the fireplace.

Carlos and Abby settled across from him, expectant looks on their faces. The rest of the small group found seats and grew quiet.

"This is for the newlyweds, but not only for them. This is for all of us who have—and still do—love. I hope you like the song."

A quiet intro was followed by the lyrics that affected her more than the first time she'd heard them in the D.C. hotel suite. She stood slightly behind Jack, her eyes closed, swaying to the music.

An intense silence followed the final strum.

"Dad, you are unbelievable. Your lyrics nailed what I feel about Abby." Carlos turned and planted a kiss on his wife's lips.

"I agree. We should have recorded you so we could listen to your gift on every anniversary," Abby said.

Jack reached into his jacket pocket and handed her a small wrapped package. "I think this may do it for you. At least until cds go the way of eight-track tapes."

"I'll download the song onto our electronic devices," Carlos said. "Will you include the song on your next album?"

He shook his head. "Some stuff should stay private."

Sally put her hand on his shoulder. "Not this, Jack. This song needs to be heard by everyone. It's for lovers of all ages, sweetie."

She raised her glass. "A toast." Waiting for everyone to find a drink, she sent a swift plea for guidance, and the right words, to her spiritual guides.

"To Carlos and Abby. May you forever hold your commitment sacred. May the love you have for each other today grow in exponential ways. And, because my son loves Mr. Spock, may you live long and prosper."

They clinked glasses and drank.

"Oh, and may you give me lots of grandchildren sooner than later."

\*\*\*\*

Jack stood, hoping he wouldn't screw up the toast he'd worked over. Now the words vanished. Time to wing it.

"My turn, and I'll second the grandchildren request." He was gratified with the laughter.

"To Abby, who kicked Carlos's butt until he called me for the first time." Over the laughter, Jack winked at his son. "Bet you didn't know she confided that little nugget. And before you start your first argument as an old married couple, let me say that I am forever indebted to both of you for having the courage I lacked.

You taught me that forgiveness is a gift worth both giving and receiving."

"I also learned that Sally raised one hell of a man." He raised his glass to her. "Here's to you, babe.

"The biggest lesson I've learned is that love endures. Sometimes when you think it's gone, when you've given up on happiness, love comes out of nowhere and kicks your butt. Finding that person who accepts you no matter what is an incredible gift. Wherever life sends me, that lesson is engraved on my heart. I hope you two never lose the gift of acceptance."

He saw Marge shifting from foot-to-foot. Her apparent nervousness surprised him, and he sent her an encouraging nod. Maybe she wasn't the bitch he'd come to expect. He hoped she'd prove him right on that count.

She held up her palm. "I wasn't sure Abigail—Abby—had made the correct choices. Sometimes we don't want our babies to grow up and move away. I'm proud of you both and look forward to spoiling grandchildren."

Abby's father glanced around the room then straightened. "To the best daughter any man could have. I know I wasn't the easiest person to live with—" he threw a look at Margaret "—but I aim to do better, starting right now." He raised his glass. "To Margaret, who gave me the best daughter in history. And to Abby, who turned out beautifully in spite of her parents. Carlos, you became my son today, but if you hurt my little girl, your ass is mine. Oh, and make that demand for grandkids unanimous."

Laughter bubbled, glasses clinked, and the group's mood lightened. Jack's mother took on the hostess role, ushering everyone into the dining room, where appetizers waited to fill hungry stomachs. The dogs followed and took up positions under the table, hoping to score off human clumsiness.

Sally disappeared into the kitchen. He followed her in to the otherwise empty room. Caging her against the countertop, he buried his nose in her neck. "Damn, you smell good."

She slid her fingers into his hair and stroked his cheekbones with her thumbs. "Likewise, I'm sure," she replied with an adenoidal voice.

"So, have you decided where you want to travel first? England, Egypt, or Peru?"

"I have somewhere much closer in mind." She smoothed her fingers over his jaw. "After all, your tour just ended. You must be sick of traveling."

He tilted his head to the side. "I'll do anything for you, babe, you know that. Just name the country and we'll head out."

"First, I'm wondering what you included in the packet you gave Carlos and Abby. It was too thick to be only a disc."

"A Christmas trip to the destination of their choice. Carlos mentioned his business drops when the kids are out on break, so I figured they might like a longer honeymoon than the one they've got planned."

Her mouth parted.

He put his finger over her lips. "I've got more money than I can spend. Besides, I put both our names on the gift. Let me do this without grousing, please."

She huffed. "I wasn't planning to grouse, I was going to tell you the gift is sweet, and I know they'll appreciate your thoughtfulness." She went up on her toes to kiss him. "Thanks for adding my name." She giggled. "I added your name to the gift I gave them, too."

He leaned back, but kept her caged. "What did you choose for the kids?"

"Tickets to the ghost tours in Asheville, Charleston, and Savannah. With paid B&B reservations and money for meals and drinks. Not that Abby will be drinking much longer."

"Well, that's—" He didn't know how to answer. "Abby, what? Do you mean she's pregnant? How do you know?"

"Not yet, but soon." She grinned. "A pixie told me."

"I'm sure you're right." Her face beamed with his words. "So, you didn't tell me. Where do you want to travel first?"

"Stratton Lake. I've seen a cottage there with a bathroom I'd maim to have as my own."

His breath stopped. "You mean you'll finally let me make an honest woman of you?"

Her eyebrows rose. "I'm already honest, but if you're referring to marriage, I'm not going there. What I mean is, once a hippie, always a hippie, but this hippie likes fluffy towels and tubs with jets. And that cottage I've seen has them both." She batted her eyelashes. "Along with a groovy hip dude who turns me on."

He leaned closer and nuzzled her ear. "Has a flower power chick like you ever considered shacking up? To get that bathroom, I mean."

"Once a hippie—"

He kissed her temples then lightly placed his lips on her closed eyelids. She sighed.

"We should follow our kid's example and get married."

She sniffed. "Okay, okay, you've made your argument. I'll live with you, and we'll see how things go. But don't get cocky. That's the only commitment I'll make."

He grinned. "You know how much I love a challenge. Especially a cocky one. I'll have you begging for more."

"We'll see."

No matter how life unwound, this was one challenge neither could lose.

**A word about the author...**

Ashantay Peters loves escaping into a well-written book. She lives in the mountains of western North Carolina, a happy transplant from the much colder (and flatter) Midwest.

She loves to hear from readers, so please contact her at ashantay.peters@gmail.com.

~*~

**Other Ashantay Peters titles**
**available from The Wild Rose Press, Inc.**
*DEATH RUB*
*DEATH STRETCH*
*DEATH UNDER THE MISTLETOE*
*DICKENS OF A DEATH*
*PIPE DREAMS*

Thank you for purchasing
this publication of The Wild Rose Press, Inc.

If you enjoyed the story, we would appreciate your
letting others know by leaving a review.

For other wonderful stories,
please visit our on-line bookstore at
www.thewildrosepress.com.

For questions or more information
contact us at
info@thewildrosepress.com.

The Wild Rose Press, Inc.
www.thewildrosepress.com

Stay current with The Wild Rose Press, Inc.

Like us on Facebook

https://www.facebook.com/TheWildRosePress

And Follow us on Twitter
https://twitter.com/WildRosePress